Cozy after Snow

AMBER KELLY

Cover Design: Sommer Stein, Perfect Pear Creative Covers
Editor: Jovana Shirley, Unforeseen Editing, www.unforeseenediting.com
Proofreader: Judy Zweifel, Judy's Proofreading
Formatter: Champagne Book Design

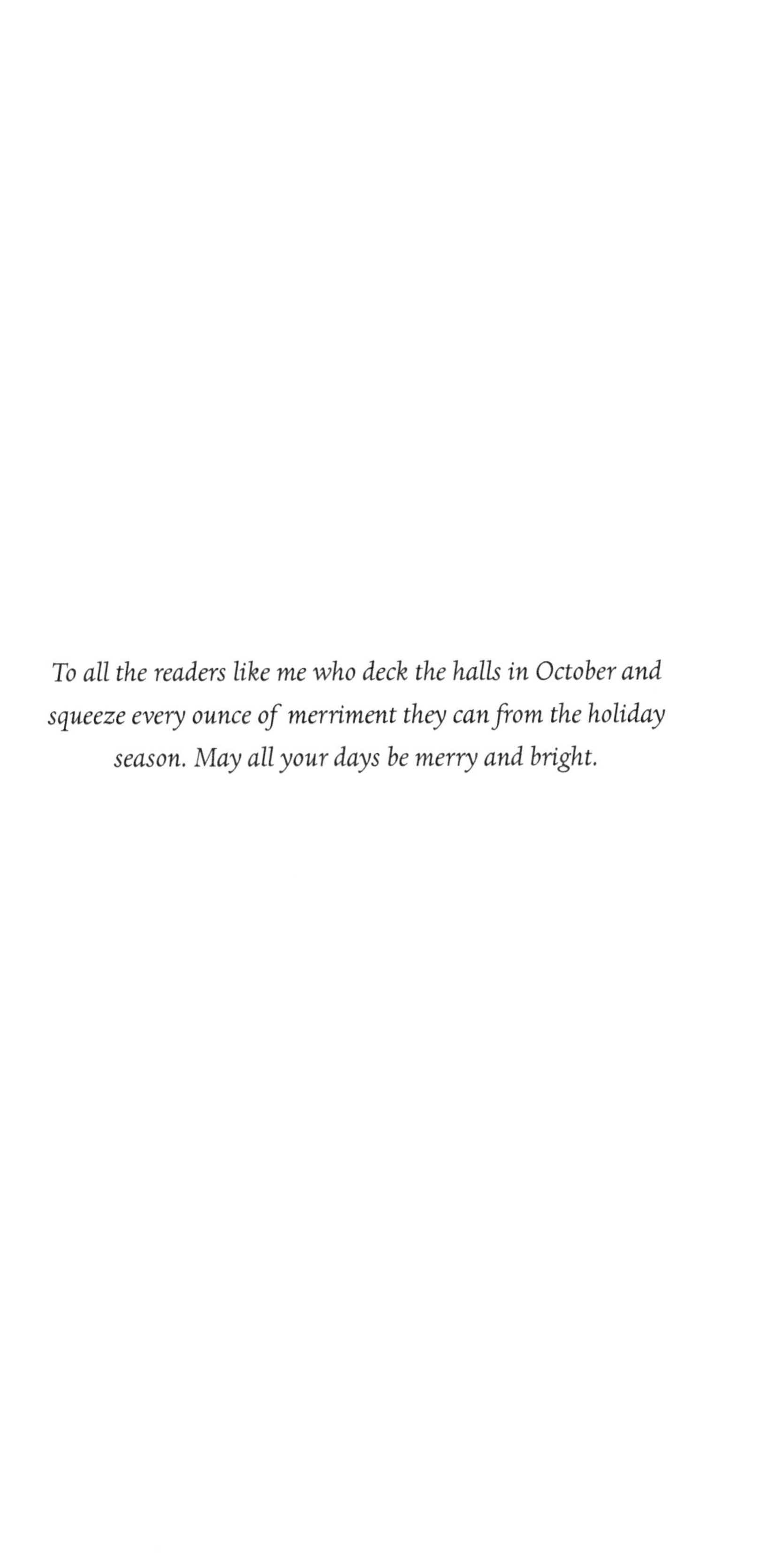

To all the readers like me who deck the halls in October and squeeze every ounce of merriment they can from the holiday season. May all your days be merry and bright.

Cozy after Snow

Chapter
one

"**G**OOD MORNING, SUNSHINE."

I awaken to the sound of Graham's voice in my ear as he begins to pull at the blankets I have wrapped tightly around me.

"No, it can't be morning yet," I mumble.

"Open your eyes," he commands.

I shake my head and burrow deeper into the covers.

"Oh, no, you don't," he says as the comforter is yanked from the bed.

"Hey," I snap as the bare skin of my legs is exposed to the coolness of the winter air.

I shoot up and spring for him.

When my body hits him, he drops the comforter and catches me as we go tumbling to the bedroom floor.

The bedroom door flings open as we land in a ball of limbs and blanket.

"Come on, guys. I'm too young to see this," Caleb cries.

I untangle myself from my husband and narrow my eyes at my son.

"You shouldn't be coming into our room, uninvited," I correct him.

He rolls his eyes. "Graham told me if he couldn't get you up and dressed in ten minutes, I had to come help him," Caleb informs.

I look from him to Graham. "You two planning to gang up on me? That's not fair," I whine as I lunge for Caleb.

I grab hold of the hem of his shirt and tug him down with us.

Then, I start peppering his face with kisses as he squirms.

"Stop it, Mom," he squeals.

Graham tackles me from behind and wrestles me to my back, where the two of them proceed to tickle me until tears are running down my cheeks.

"I give up," I gasp through the giggles.

"You going to get up and get dressed now?" Caleb asks.

"Yes, I promise," I agree.

He hops up, and Graham follows. Then, Graham extends a hand to help me.

"You jump in the shower, and we'll make you breakfast," he says as he hoists me to my feet.

"Then, we're going to get a Christmas tree!" Caleb bellows.

That's right. I forgot. Today is December 1, and we told Caleb we'd spend today at the Christmas tree lot in the valley, picking out the perfect tree, and then we'd decorate it tonight before he leaves for Chicago in the morning to spend a week with his father and baby brother for the holidays.

I don't want him to go. I want him to be here with us to help decorate the rest of the house for our first Christmas as a new family, but it's Damon's turn to have him for Christmas, and he graciously agreed to let Caleb spend it in Balsam Ridge so he could attend his uncle Garrett's wedding on Christmas Eve. So, we'll have to make the most of today and tonight.

I shuffle into the bathroom while they head to the kitchen.

I shower quickly and decide to let my hair air dry. I swipe on some moisturizer and lip balm and spritz on a little perfume.

Searching the walk-in closet, I find a warm Christmas sweater and a pair of fleece-lined leggings. Once I'm dressed, I slide into a pair of black UGG boots and go in search of my boys.

I find them at the stove. Graham is flipping pancakes as Caleb watches a pan of sizzling bacon.

It's a beautiful sight.

"Something smells delicious," I say as I make my way to the island.

Caleb glances over his shoulder. "We made gingerbread pancakes."

"Gingerbread? My favorite," I coo.

Caleb moves the bacon to a paper towel–covered plate, and then he pulls three glasses from the cabinet above the microwave and fills them with milk.

Graham loads us each a plate with three pancakes and three crispy strips while I fetch the maple syrup from the cupboard.

"Are you guys excited to pick a tree?" I ask as we dig into our meal.

Caleb nods enthusiastically and answers around a mouthful of pancakes. "Graham said we could get the biggest one on the lot."

"The biggest one?" I ask as I slide my eyes to Graham.

"Yep, we have to get there before Tucker though," Caleb quips.

Tucker is our nephew and Caleb's best friend.

"Why's that?" I ask.

"Because he said he and his dad were going to get the biggest."

"So, that's why you two sneak-attacked me so early," I accuse.

Caleb looks at Graham and grins.

"Devils. You're lucky these pancakes are so good that I have to forgive you." I pop a bite into my mouth.

Once we've cleaned our plates, Graham goes to warm up his truck as I clean our dishes.

A gentle snowfall garnishes the pines as we make our way down the mountain toward Merry Ridge Tree Farm.

We wind our way down the drive that leads to the parking lot, which is already full of trucks.

People are milling around the entrance with cups in their glove-covered hands.

There is a small building with a window to the right. The sign above it says *Hot Cocoa and Warm Cider*.

Two men—dressed in jeans, flannels, and boots—are operating a tree baler, where a family is standing, waiting for their pick to be netted and loaded into their vehicle.

Christmas music envelops us as we pile out of the truck and make our way forward.

Graham takes my hand and leads the way as we trudge through the freshly fallen snow, our breath visible in the crisp winter air. The aroma of pine surrounds us as we venture deeper into the tree farm, Caleb by our side.

My eyes scan the rows of evergreens. Each tree is special in its own way, waiting to be chosen to grace a home for the joyous season.

When we come to a patch of impressive-sized options, Caleb runs ahead of us and examines tree after tree, looking for the one that rises above the rest.

"Over here," he calls, and we follow his voice to a towering Fraser fir.

The tree is magnificent, lush, and full, its needles a vibrant shade of green.

"Um, Caleb, that's a bit too high," I mutter as I take in the giant fir that reaches proudly toward the sky.

"No, it's perfect," he insists.

Graham lets go of my hand and walks over to Caleb. His hand coming to my son's shoulder. They both stare up at the top of the branches.

"I think you're right," Graham agrees, "but we'd better measure it to make sure."

I shake my head as he produces a tape measure from his pocket.

"Sixteen feet, give or take an inch," he assesses.

"Will it fit?" Caleb asks.

"We might have to trim a little off the top, but I believe you found the one," Graham says as he takes the long stick with a yellow flag on the top that Caleb snatched from a barrel as we entered the farm and raises it high in the air and waves.

A few moments later, two men arrive on a quad that has a long trailer attached to the back with a chain saw in hand.

"You want to do the honors?" one of them asks Caleb, whose eyes go round and then comes to me.

"Can I?"

"Yes, just be careful and let Graham help you," I say.

He takes the saw in his hand, and Graham shows him how to crank it as the workers tie a thin rope around the middle of the trunk.

The sound of the saw echoes through the forest as Graham guides Caleb to the ground. As they cut through the base, the two men pull the rope and guide it down, clear of them.

"That was so cool," Caleb cries as he turns to me. "Mom, I cut down our Christmas tree!"

I smile at him. "I see that. Good job," I praise.

The four of them load the tree onto the trailer, and we follow on foot as they haul it back to the entrance of the farm.

A line has formed at the baler, so I walk over and purchase us all a large Styrofoam cup of cocoa while we wait our turn.

A pair of arms wraps around me from behind, and I look down to see Tucker's face grinning up at me.

"Hey, Aunt Taeli." He beams.

"Hi yourself, handsome."

I add three more cups to my order, and he helps me haul them over to where his dad, Langford, and his stepmother, Isley, have joined my boys, and we hand them out.

"Looks like you guys found a fine tree," Langford says.

"Yep, the biggest one they had," Caleb says.

"Ah, man," Tucker gripes.

Graham reaches over and ruffles his nephew's hair. "I'm sure if you look hard enough, you'll find one just as tall."

He looks over to his brother and mouths, *Sixteen.*

Langford nods.

Caleb breaks away and walks toward one of the big oak barrels.

"What do you think you're doing?" I call.

He stops and turns to me in confusion. "I'm returning the flag," he says.

"Oh, no, you don't. We aren't finished," I quip.

He furrows his brows. "We aren't?"

"No, sir. I want a tree for my bedroom and one for your bedroom and one for the dining room, oh, and one for the porch," I say, ticking each one off on my fingers.

"Are you serious? Four more trees?" he asks as his eyes snap to Graham's.

Graham shrugs. "I guess you'd better get to looking, but no more sixteen-footers. Let's keep these to about six feet."

Caleb lets out an excited yell, and he and Tucker run off among the trees.

Langford looks at Isley. "You're gonna make me cut down five trees now, too, aren't you?"

Her mouth curls up on one end.

"Shit, I should have brought the big truck," he says before stomping off after the boys.

Isley follows as I wait in line with Graham.

Once the beast of a tree is netted, he helps one of the farmers carry it to our truck.

As he lowers the tailgate and they secure it to the bed, I know we have found the perfect Christmas tree, one that will be the centerpiece of our holiday celebrations as a new family.

I stop and take in the moment of pure magic.

"You okay?" Graham asks, pulling me from my thoughts.

I smile up at him. "Better than okay. I'm so happy; I could burst. This is going to be the best Christmas ever," I whisper.

He wraps an arm around my shoulders and kisses the top of my head. "Good. That's what I was shooting for. Now, let's go find the kiddos and get these additional trees picked out so we can get home."

I can't wrap my head around how much life has changed in these past few years. I could be back in Illinois, sitting on the country club's planning committee, arguing over what theme this year's holiday ball should reflect. Dieting so I'd fit perfectly into an extravagant cocktail dress while secretly wishing I could eat all the Christmas cookies. Acting surprised when I opened yet another ridiculously expensive, impersonal piece of jewelry Damon had had his secretary pick out and wrap for me to make up for his absence and lack of cheer and avoiding my mother's call that would inevitably fill me with guilt.

I used to dread the season. Now, I can't wait to celebrate with my big, beautiful, new family and friends.

Bringing Caleb to Balsam Ridge was the best decision I've ever made.

Life after failing as a wife the first time sure is sweet.

Chapter
two

Graham

WE COMPROMISED. ONE LARGE TREE FOR THE LIVING ROOM, one six-footer for the deck, and two three-footers for the bedrooms. And those barely fit in the back of the pickup. Langford laughed as he helped me load them, but I got the last laugh as Tucker and Isley chose four massive trees of their own.

"What the hell do we need all those for? We aren't even gonna be at the house on Christmas morning. We'll all be at the resort," he asks me as we watch our wives and sons fawn over the evergreens.

I shrug. "If it makes them that happy, I'll put a tree in every open space of the house," I muse.

His eyes slide to me. "Yeah, me too. Crazy women."

The boys get in line for the sleigh ride through the pines.

I smile to myself as I watch them chatting animatedly, clutching the Styrofoam cups of chocolaty goodness, with the other waiting kids. Mom and Pop brought my brothers and me here to pick out a tree every year. We'd ride the sleigh and sing carols, drink cider, and eat cookies.

"How cool is it, watching our kids experience the same things we did, growing up?" I ask Langford.

"Pretty fucking awesome," he agrees.

Taeli finds us in the parking lot.

"Look at what we just found in the gift shop," Taeli says, holding up a long-sleeved maternity tee that says *Santa Baby* with a Santa hat over the words.

"Are you trying to tell me something?" I ask.

"No, I got it for Isley," she says.

"And what else did you get?" I ask as I eye the large brown bag in her hand.

"A couple of ornaments, a sprig of mistletoe, a make-your-own garland kit, and a few gingerbread houses for the boys to assemble. Oh, and this is for you." She pulls a sweater from the bag.

It's red and white, and it reads *The Jolliest Bunch of Assholes This Side of the Nuthouse*. A quote from the best Christmas movie ever made.

"What do you think?" she asks, her eyes glistening with excitement.

I take the sweater from her fingers and hold it up to my chest.

"I love it," I declare, and she beams.

"God, I hope Isley doesn't end up in that shop," Langford mumbles.

Taeli's eyes snap to him. "She's checking out now."

"Shit. We'll probably end up with matching sweaters," he groans.

He doesn't mind one bit. I know my older brother. I can read it in his eyes and hear it in his voice. He loves every second of this. It's just been him and Tuck for a long time, and while he did his best to make sure his son had a wonderful holiday experience, he could never quite create the magic that Isley inevitably will.

I glance at my wife.

It's the same for me. I didn't realize how empty my house, my life, was until Taeli and Caleb came barreling in and made it a home.

"We should have an ugly Christmas sweater party!" Taeli squeals.

Langford huffs. "When? Between us busing the boys to their other parent's homes, preparing for Garrett's Hollywood-style wedding, the valley Christmas parade, and creating Santa's Village at the ski resort on Misty Mountain, we're running low on time already. Isley's been distraught because we have no time in the schedule this year to visit her brother and parents in Arizona."

"Can't you at least send her?" I ask.

"Alone? Fuck no. She's too far along in the pregnancy. I wouldn't want her to travel that far without me to help. Besides, she's the mayor, so she needs to be there for the parade and town festivities, and she doesn't want to miss the wedding."

"That sucks. She needs to see her dad," Taeli utters.

Langford's father-in-law suffers from Alzheimer's, and as the disease progresses, his memory and cognitive functions are diminishing.

"I know," Langford whispers.

I place a hand on his shoulder and squeeze.

"Try not to stress about any of it, bro. If you get caught up in all the regrets of what you can't do, it'll overshadow the joy in what you can. Just make it the best Christmas for Isley and Tucker that you can and enjoy the hell out of it," I suggest.

"Yeah," he mutters.

Isley emerges from the front of the gift shop with both arms loaded down with purchases.

The corner of Langford's mouth lifts as he shakes his head. "Crazy woman."

He goes to help his wife with her bags, and Taeli sets hers in the back of the truck and turns to me. She wraps her arms around my neck.

"How about a romantic sleigh ride through the snowy pines with your wife and a dozen loud, sticky kids?"

I kiss the tip of her frozen nose. "Sounds perfect."

After our ride with the kids, we head home to begin decking the halls.

I park the truck in front of our modern Swiss chalet, and Taeli hurries inside with her bags as Caleb and I unload and trim the trees.

We enter our cozy mountain home, the scent of pine and the warmth of the crackling fire greeting us, and carefully deposit the trees in stands and place them in the spots assigned by Taeli.

The massive sixteen-foot Christmas tree stands in the corner of our spacious living room beside the stone fireplace, its branches stretching toward and nearly reaching the ceiling. The thought of decorating it is a mix of joy and challenge as I fetch the A-frame ladder from the garage.

"All right, team," Taeli says with enthusiasm, "let's make this tree the best decorated in Balsam Ridge."

Caleb glances at me and rolls his eyes as we gather around the tree, plastic totes of ornaments and twinkling lights spread out across the floor.

"This is going to take all night," Caleb muses.

Taeli looks up from the ball of lights she is trying to untangle. "It's a good thing I called in reinforcements."

As if on cue, the front door swings open, and Taeli's mother, Leona, and her beau, Ralph Gentry, enter, their arms loaded down with boxes.

"Granna," Caleb cries as he runs to Leona. "Look at our Christmas tree." He points up at the Fraser fir.

"Wow, that's a stunner," Leona gasps.

"Yeah, thank goodness you came by because we're gonna need a lot of help to decorate it," Caleb quips.

"Well, we brought dinner so we can get our bellies full and get to it," Ralph says.

Caleb takes the box from his grandmother's grasp and follows Ralph into the kitchen.

"Sara-Beth and Hilton are coming by to pitch in as well. I talked to her on the ride over, and they'll be here as soon as they finish up at Langford's," Leona informs us.

"They don't have to rush over here. I'm sure Isley can use the help too," I say.

"Zoey and Morris are over there. Besides, Sara-Beth and Hilton want to see Caleb before he leaves for Chicago."

I see the sadness flash in Taeli's eyes before she can hide it.

It's always difficult for her to send Caleb to his father's, but this time of year is especially hard because there is much he will miss.

Caleb and Ralph rejoin us, and before long, the ladies retreat to the kitchen to get dinner heated and plated while we fellas get to work, twisting the lights around the tree.

Mom and Pop arrive, and we share the meal of pot roast and cornbread with them before we return to the task at hand.

The room echoes with laughter as Caleb and I engage in a friendly competition to see who can empty a tote and get the ornaments on the tree fastest while Taeli, Mom, and Leona sit, threading popcorn and cranberries and critiquing our placement skills.

"Caleb, you have to spread them out better than that. All your balls are in a clump," Taeli instructs.

"It's no fair. He's taller than me," Caleb cries.

Ralph quietly makes his way to Caleb's side and starts sneakily moving ornaments up higher.

I watch as Caleb grins when his soon-to-be grandfather winks at him.

We cover the branches with the delicate glass ornaments Taeli purchased with beautiful, intricate designs and mix in Caleb's hand-made creations from school years past.

I contribute some old-fashioned wooden ornaments from my first marriage. Taeli found the box I had saved in the attic, and when I explained what they were, she insisted we keep and display them.

Once we've emptied all the totes, Pop turns off the lights, and I climb under the tree and secure the plug in the outlet.

As the lights come to life, bathing the room in a warm and magical glow, I help Taeli carefully climb the ladder and secure the star atop the tree. A reminder of the Star of Bethlehem that guided the three kings to baby Jesus.

Caleb claps his hands in delight. "It's the best tree we've ever had," he exclaims.

"It is perfect," Taeli says.

I pick the green-and-red bag up from its hiding place behind the sofa.

"Not quite," I say as I hand it over to Taeli.

She gives me a curious look. "What's this?"

"Open it," I prompt.

She plucks the white tissue paper, tosses it aside, and gasps as she tugs the red ribbon, revealing a white farmhouse ornament with a wooden tag hanging from the bottom that reads *Our First Christmas 2023*.

She turns to Leona, her eyes filled with tears. "It's the ornament Daddy made for you," she whispers.

"Yes, he carved it and painted it himself. He had the cuts on his hands to prove it," Leona says.

"I added the new tag on the bottom, the one with the original date," I explain.

Taeli lifts the model in the air, reads the date of her parents' first Christmas together, and shakes her head. "I can't take this. He made it for you, Mom."

Leona walks over and covers her hand that's holding the ornament. "He would want you to have it. It's time for you to hang it on your tree to signify your new beginning. So he'll always be a part of your celebrations. He'd be so happy that you found your way home."

Taeli collapses in her mother's arms, and they let the tears flow before they place the ornament front and center together.

Pop shares stories of his own as we move on to the other rooms and continue to decorate, reminiscing about the Christmases I celebrated with my parents and brothers when we were boys.

Taeli and I stand back and watch as Caleb listens intently with his eyes wide and a smile that stretches from ear to ear.

He looks back at us and says, "Can we go sledding Christmas morning too?"

"Sure, buddy," I answer.

"This is going to be the best Christmas ever!"

"It definitely is," Taeli agrees.

Our first Christmas together under this roof is something we have all been eagerly anticipating, and as I take in their joyful faces, it's a reminder of the beauty of new beginnings, the power of love, and the magic of the seasons.

I'm filled with gratitude for the memories we're creating and the love that binds us together.

My family.

Jena

I PICK ERIN UP, AND THE TWO OF US HEAD TO OUR BEST FRIEND, Ansley's, shop in Market Square—Well-Bred Café and Bookstore—where all the girls are meeting tonight for our last official hurrah before the big day.

Ansley, Erin, and I have been friends since we were little girls. We've seen each other through all of life's big events. The two of them were in my wedding, and Ansley and I were in both of Erin's.

Our girl gang has grown exponentially over the past few years, and we couldn't be happier.

We never thought the day would come when we'd get to celebrate Ansley's nuptials, but that devil Garrett Tuttle, her high school sweetheart, popped back up in Balsam Ridge and swept her right off her feet.

Truth be told, we always knew the two of them would eventually find their way back to one another.

We stop to pick up the pizza order that Taeli called in earlier, and when we arrive, everyone is already settled in with a glass of wine in hand, so we pour ourselves a glass and join them.

"It feels like I've been waiting for this day forever, and now, it's three weeks away," Ansley says as her mother passes out the boxes holding our bridesmaid dresses.

Our last fitting was just before Thanksgiving, and the boutique finished the final alterations this past weekend.

Sara-Beth, Erin, Taeli, and I closed the Rocky Pass office early yesterday and made the four-hour drive out to Nashville to pick them up, along with Ansley's handmade wedding gown, a gorgeous custom piece designed for her with the silk from the dress her mother had worn the day her parents were married.

"Come on. Let's try these babies on one last time," Erin says as she stands and pulls her sweater over her head.

"Erin, people can see in here," I cry.

She turns to see the blinds are still open and shrugs. "The parking lot is empty. Besides, if a man wanders by who's never seen a girl in a bra before, he can thank me later."

I hurry to the front of the store and quickly pull the blinds closed. "Children are walking around, looking at the valley Christmas lights with their families," I hiss.

"Oops," she mutters.

Once the windows are covered, we all undress and step into the gorgeous, sleeveless, candy-cane-red-hued chiffon cowl-neck frocks.

They hug our hips and have a pleated slit on the left that comes up to our mid-thigh.

"Ansley, don't you want to try on yours?" I ask.

She shakes her head. "I don't want to risk ripping it or spilling anything on it," she says.

She's been a nervous wreck since she and Garrett signed a deal to allow *Country Today* exclusive access to the wedding.

Garrett and his team felt that it was for the best. They announced the deal months ahead of the wedding in hopes that overzealous paparazzi wouldn't go out of their way to crash the nuptials, expecting a big payday from gossip magazines vying to scoop each other. They picked the outlet for the publication of the first photos of their big day, and all the proceeds made from the large contract will be donated to St. Jude's Children's Research Hospital.

It is brilliant, but I hate seeing Ansley fret over everything being perfect.

I march over to the stool her gown is perched on, pick it up, and unzip the bag.

"What are you doing?" Ansley asks.

"Helping you into your gown," I say.

"I don't want to—"

I cut her off, "Yes, you do. You're letting that magazine story steal your joy, and I won't have it. Now, strip," I demand.

She sighs.

I raise an eyebrow.

"Fine, but everyone set their wineglasses behind the counter," she huffs and kicks her loafers off.

They all gather the crystal and do as instructed, and I wait patiently as she strips down to her undies. Then, her mother and Sara-Beth help her step into the gown.

It fits her perfectly.

She twirls, and the skirt of the whimsical silk ball gown with a Chantilly lace bodice and delicate frosted beading flares, exposing the layers of tulle underneath.

"Oh, Ansley, it's exquisite," Anna bellows.

"Absolutely stunning," Isley agrees.

"It has a detachable train so I don't have to change in order to dance at the reception," she says.

"You look like a freaking princess," I praise.

Ansley beams at us all.

"Do you guys want to see the shoes?" she asks.

"Hell yeah," I answer for us all.

She gathers the sides of the gown in her fists and turns to run upstairs to her apartment.

When she returns, she is carrying a box that reads *Badgley Mischka*.

"These came in last week, and I've been dying to show you guys," she says as she sets the box on the counter and lifts the top.

Tucked inside is a pair of Tiffany-blue satin stiletto heels with vintage pearl embellishments.

"I had them special ordered. They are my something blue."

"Oh, Ansley. They're magnificent," Taeli utters.

"I have something for you guys too," Ansley says.

"Us?" I ask.

She grins at me. "Yes, you didn't think I forgot about the bridesmaid gifts, did you?"

Her mother hands her a wooden box filled with little blue boxes, and she passes us each two apiece.

Inside is a pair of pearl earrings with a matching open-heart pearl bracelet.

"Do you guys like them?" she asks as we all tug them loose and start to put them on.

"Are you kidding?" I ask.

"They're gorgeous," Anna says.

"And they fit, unlike this dress," Maxi adds.

We all turn to her.

"What? Your dress doesn't fit?" Ansley squeals.

Maxi's eyes shoot to her. "No, it does. It's just a little snug."

"There's no time to send it back," Ansley says, panic rising in her voice.

Maxi puts her hands on her hips. "Calm down. I'll just lay off dessert and cocktails for a couple of weeks. It's not a big deal."

"Are you sure?"

"Yeah, I'm sure. It's not bad. I just don't want a boob to pop out on the dance floor and end up on the cover of *Country Daily*," Maxi quips.

Anna looks down at her chest. "I think they're supposed to fit like that. My girls are on full display too."

Ansley's brows furrow as she takes us all in, and Erin steps forward to defuse the situation.

"Hey, if anybody is stealing the spotlight and upstaging the bride and groom, it will be me and Jena doing the worm across the dance floor in this thing," she snaps as she wiggles her hips.

Ansley's eyes go wide. "You guys wouldn't."

"Play some Vanilla Ice and see what happens," I dare.

"Oh, 'Ice Ice Baby' is on the playlist," she assures us.

"We have another gift," Ansley's mother calls.

"Right. I almost forgot," Ansley says as she reaches behind the counter and pulls out two large white bags.

Inside is a package for each of us with our names printed on the top.

I bring it to my ear and shake. "What is it?" I ask.

"Open it," she urges.

We all lift the lid in unison and find a pair of pink silk pajamas with the word *bridesmaid* embroidered on the back.

"Wow, fancy," Erin says as she holds the top up.

"I have a white pair that says *bride*, and Mom, Sara-Beth, and Leona have ivory."

"You shouldn't have. You already sprang for the jewelry," I tell her.

"I didn't. The magazine is going to photograph us getting ready before the wedding and thought it'd be nice if we were all in matching outfits. The designer partnered with them and gifted the entire bridal party with these. There are robes and slippers for each of us as well. Oh, and, Jena, I have a set, along with earrings, for Annabelle," she explains.

My daughter, Annabelle, is her flower girl.

"She'll love that," I say.

"We should have told them they could photograph you on the honeymoon. You'd have gotten a whole new free designer wardrobe," Erin says as she slides her arms into the pajama top.

"God, no. It's enough to have them at the wedding. I'd like to relax and enjoy my honeymoon. Thank you."

"Where are you two going?" Anna asks.

"Home," Ansley says, her voice a blissful sigh.

"Home?" I question.

She looks at me and grins. "Yep, we get four luxurious weeks alone at our new home that we've yet to spend any time in since it's been completed."

"You mean you could go anywhere in the world you want to go for four weeks and you chose here?" I squeak.

She nods. "Absolutely, and we can't wait."

It makes sense. Garrett is a musician who has been on a world-wide tour, promoting his latest album. Ansley has flown out to meet him at a couple of stops, so of course, they prefer to settle in and spend quality time at the new mansion on the mountain he had built for them.

"And we are looking forward to having Garrett around for a while," Sara-Beth adds.

I lean in to whisper to Ansley, "You'd better lock the gate and turn your phones off."

"Oh, we will," she agrees.

We all carefully remove our dresses and return them to their bags while Sara-Beth and Ansley's mother, Mrs. Humphries, help Ansley out of her gown.

Once all of the formalwear is secured, Erin passes us back our glasses, and we dig into the pizza.

The rest of the evening is spent laughing and crying and enjoying each other.

I'm so lucky to have this group of fierce women in my life, and I am overjoyed that my daughter has them in her life as well. I pray she finds a tribe this amazing one day.

Chapter
four

Maxi

I LOOK AROUND THE LIVING AREA AND KITCHEN FOR THE KEYS, which are in my hand.

Geezus, Maxi. You're losing it.

A yawn escapes me, and I decide to sit for a moment and catch my bearings before I leave for work.

My eyes scan the room.

The tree Langford and Morris brought over from the tree lot last night is leaning in the corner. I intended to get up early today and go shopping for supplies to decorate it, but I just couldn't rally.

I'll stop on the way to the brewery. I have plenty of time.

I cover another yawn with the back of my hand, lean my head against the back of the sofa, and close my eyes for a moment.

Ring.

I blink my eyes open and look around the dark room in confusion.

The sound starts again. I pat around me, searching for the source of the noise, fish my phone from between the sofa cushions, and bring it to my ear.

"Hello?" I rasp.

"Did you send me the pictures of Momma for Cara's school project?"

My sister, Lynn's, impatient voice greets me.

Crap.

My niece is doing a Christmas project at school that includes a collage of generational family photos. Lynn asked me if I had any of our mother when she was a girl. I found several of her with our grandparents when I went through her things. I was supposed to mail them to Lynn last week.

"I forgot. I'm so sorry," I admit groggily.

She sighs. "It's fine. I only sent you two reminders this week, but whatever. I'll just have her draw a few stick figures into the collage to represent a couple of generations," she snaps.

It's clearly not fine.

"Sis, I said I'm sorry. I'll get them to the post office first thing in the morning and send them express," I promise.

She doesn't respond.

"Lynn?"

"That'll work. It's not like you," she mutters.

"I know. I don't know what's wrong with me. I've just been so damn tired lately," I whine as I look at the clock on the microwave.

Is it really eight o'clock?

"Tired? Why?" she asks.

I can hear the slight panic in her voice. When our mother started suffering from suspicious exhaustion, it was the first sign something was very wrong.

"Don't worry. I'm not sick or anything. I'm just off. And my bladder isn't helping. I swear I have to pee half a dozen times at night even if I cut myself off from all liquids early in the evening. It's messing with my sleep."

I was supposed to be at work over an hour ago. I place Lynn on speaker and click over to text my boss, Reed, and find I have several worried texts from him.

Sorry I'm late. Wasn't feeling well and fell asleep. Didn't see your messages. Heading your way now.

Where are my damn keys?

"Tired? Frequent urination? Sounds to me like you're pregnant," she quips.

"What? No. That's not possible."

I check the incoming message as she continues.

"Are you telling me that you and that hunky fireman of yours aren't making the headboard rattle on the regular?" she asks.

No problem. I could tell you weren't yourself last night. I'll cover your shift. Take a sick day and get some rest. I'll see you tomorrow.

"Of course we are, but we're careful," I tell her.

"Careful how exactly?"

"We use protection," I mutter as I type out a reply.

Thanks, Reed. I'll make it up to you.

"Use your words, Maxi. What kind of protection?" she pushes.

"Condoms."

"Well, there you go. Condoms aren't always reliable. Trust me, I know," she says.

"They've always been reliable for me," I state.

"And you two have never ever fooled around without one? Not once?" she questions.

I hesitate.

"Maxi?"

"A few times, okay? In the shower, but he pulls out every time," I explain.

She laughs. "Oh my God, just go to the pharmacy and buy a pregnancy test."

"Why?" I squeal.

I don't squeal. What the fuck is wrong with me?

"So you know for sure," she insists.

"You just told me I couldn't trust condoms from the pharmacy. Why the hell should I trust a piece of plastic that you pee on to tell me whether or not my life is about to drastically change?" I shout.

"Breathe, Maxi," Lynn coaxes.

"Breathe? Are you fucking kidding me right now?" I screech out.

"You're going to hyperventilate. That won't be good for the baby."

"Lynn!" I scream into the phone.

More laughter.

"I'm sorry. I'm yanking your chain. It's too fun," she says.

"It's not fun for me," I bite.

"Seriously, Maxi. It can't hurt to get a test. If it's negative, you can write it all off to stress or something."

Stress. That's it.

"Stress. Oh my God, yes," I say in relief.

"I've never known you to stress about anything," she points out.

"I usually don't, but Corbin has been gone the last week. Valley Fire and Rescue was called out to help fight a wildfire that blazed out of control in Montana," I explain.

"A wildfire in December? Isn't that kind of strange?" she asks.

"Not really. According to Corbin, their fire season was extended due to a record drought and unseasonably warm temperatures for the state. They've had to deal with several grassland fires this year, and the latest one got out of control. Lots of people have lost their homes and businesses."

"This close to Christmas? That's horrible," Lynn murmurs.

"Yeah, ten thousand acres burned before they got it contained. Thank goodness no lives were lost, and he and the guys are heading home later this evening," I say.

"I guess that would stress me out too," she sympathizes.

"That and the fact that I've been dieting. I'm fucking hangry," I growl.

"You, dieting? What the hell for?" she asks.

"Ansley and Garrett's wedding. Our stupid bridesmaid dresses came in a couple of days ago, and I swear I can barely breathe in the thing. So, I swore off all sweets, sodas, and alcohol until the reception, and then they'd better hope they get a chance to cut the wedding cake before I tackle it and drink a small fortune's worth of whiskey at the open bar," I rant.

"A snug dress, you say?"

Shit.

"The dress shop messed up the alterations; even Anna was complaining about her fit," I reason.

"Uh-huh. Go get a test and call me back," she demands.

"Whatever."

I click off the line and go in search of my freaking keys.

I pace around the living room, staring at the timer on my phone.

This has to be the longest three minutes of my life.

When the alarm chimes, I sprint to the bathroom, where the five tests I purchased are lined up on the counter.

My hand trembles as I pick up the first one.

One pink line.

One.

I fish one of the discarded boxes from the wastebasket and read the directions again. One line equals not pregnant. Two lines equal pregnant.

Slumping down onto the toilet seat, I take a deep breath as disappointment washes over me.

Wait, what? Disappointment?

No. Not disappointment. Relief. It has to be relief.

I shake my head to clear my thoughts. This is a good thing. No, this is a great thing. I have no business being anyone's mother. I'm not a nurturer. I work in a brewery. I drive a motorcycle, break up bar fights, and get hangry when I have to skip dessert, for goodness' sake.

Corbin and I haven't even talked about marriage yet, much less having a baby.

This is good.

Then, why does my chest ache?

I stand and wipe my eyes.

You're being silly, Maxi.

I berate myself as I pick up the waste bin and start to swipe all the tests into it. Then, my eye catches sight of one of the tiny windows that has two lines.

Two.

I pull each of them back out and look at them. Three with two bold lines. One with two faint lines.

The first one is still perched on the back of the toilet. I sit and examine it more closely.

One bold line and one very faint one.

Positive. All five are positive.

My hand drops to my stomach as the news sinks in.

I'm gonna be a mother.

Me.

I'm shocked by the tears of joy that leak down my cheeks.

I shouldn't want this. I have no business wanting this.

But I want this.

I hope Corbin wants this.

I dispose of the tests and walk out of the bathroom and into our bedroom, where my phone is charging.

Clicking Lynn's name, I bring the phone to my ear.

"Well, am I about to be the best aunt who's ever lived or what?"

"Yes," I mutter.

The line goes silent.

"Lynn?"

I hear her sniffle before she replies, her voice cracking, "Did you say yes?"

"Yes, I'm pregnant," I admit.

"Yes!" she roars, and I have to pull the phone from my ear.

"Jeez, calm down. I think you scared the baby," I tease.

"I can't believe it. I know I convinced you to take a test, but I didn't actually think it would be positive. I was mostly messing with you. This is the best Christmas present ever!"

"You're welcome," I deadpan.

"Have you told Corbin?"

"No. I found out five minutes ago, and he is on an airplane. When would I have told him?"

"Ah, so I'm the first one you told?" she murmurs.

I can hear the surprise in her voice, and I know that it means a lot to her.

"I was the first one you told you were expecting Cara," I say.

"Yeah, but I was a knocked-up teenager who was still in high school and scared shitless to tell Jim or our mother."

"So, I told Momma for you," I recall.

"Yep, and I told Jim at the football game that Friday night, and he passed out in the bleachers and ended up with a concussion."

We both laugh.

"Hopefully, Corbin will take the news better," I quip.

"Oh, Maxi, I'm sure he'll be thrilled. Momma would be too, you know," she states.

"I wish she were here," I whisper.

"Me too, but, hey, you and that baby aren't going to be short on love. You've got me and the entire Tuttle family," she imparts.

It's true. This baby will be blessed.

"Thanks, sis. I think I'm going to go lie down for a while before Corbin gets home."

"Call me the minute you tell him," she demands.

"I will," I promise.

"I love you."

"Love you more," I say before ending the call.

I cradle my tummy and whisper, "Come on, kiddo. Let's go rest before Daddy gets home."

I know it's probably too soon, but I swear I feel an excited flutter.

I STEP OUT OF THE TRUCK AND LET OUT A SIGH OF RELIEF AS THE fresh, cool mountain air hits me.

It was a long week. The fires in Montana put up a hell of a fight. One small town was basically leveled. The devastation multiplied, being as it's so close to Christmas.

Thank goodness no lives were lost.

We do our best to protect and save homes and businesses, but in the end, the lives are the only things that matter.

Everything else can be replaced or rebuilt.

I grab my gear from the bed of the truck and head toward the entrance to the house, surprised but elated to see Maxi's car is still here. When we spoke yesterday, I thought she had said she had to work tonight.

I wanted to ask her to call out because having her in my arms is the best medicine after a grueling fight with Mother Nature.

Looks like she read my mind.

I enter through the side door and kick my boots off in the mud-room, then go in search of my girl.

I find her curled up on the couch with a pillow behind her head and a knitted blanket tucked under her chin. Her face is obscured by her long, dark hair, and I can hear the faint snore.

She is out.

I set my bag on the kitchen island before I quietly make my way to her side.

Leaning down, I brush a lock from her face and lay a kiss on her forehead.

She smiles in her sleep, and I swear it's the sexiest damn thing I've ever seen.

I kiss her again, this time moving down to the corner of her mouth.

Her eyes blink open.

"Hey," I whisper.

"Hey."

She smiles at me for a few more beats before her eyes widen and she sits straight up.

"You're home. Oh my goodness, I must have fallen asleep hard. What time is it?"

"A little past nine," I answer.

"Nine!" she shouts, jolting up to her feet.

I watch her fidget for a moment, amused.

"Corbin," she begins, her voice trembling with nerves.

I stand and wait, her big brown eyes meeting mine, and I smile, trying to gauge what has her on edge.

Is it the fire?

"I have something to tell you," she continues.

"Okay."

I take a seat on the sofa as she paces in front of me.

"Baby, whatever it is, just spill it, and we'll work through it," I say.

She stops mid-stride and looks at me. Fear is written all over her.

What the hell is wrong?

Fighting the urge to reach out and pull her to me, I wait silently for her to start talking, and when she finally does, it knocks me for a loop.

"I … I'm pregnant."

Her whispered words hang in the air as a range of emotions hit me all at once. Surprise, disbelief, and then an overwhelming sense of wonder and joy.

"Pregnant?" I repeat.

She nods.

"Are you serious?"

"As a heart attack," she mutters.

She stands before me, wringing her hands as she waits for me to respond.

A baby.

"Cor? Say something," she pleads.

I don't. I can't. Instead, I drop to my knees in front of her, and she takes a startled step backward.

"What are you doing? Don't you fucking dare propose to me right now, Corbin Tuttle. I can only handle one life-altering event at a time," she shrieks.

My forehead drops to her stomach as I wrap my arms around her waist.

She threads her fingers into my hair as I begin to shake with emotion.

"Are those happy tears or *what the fuck did we do* tears?" she asks, apprehension clear in her voice.

I look up at her. "I'm gonna be a dad. That's the best welcome home I've ever received. Fuck, Maxi, I couldn't be happier," I tell her.

"Really?"

"All I've ever wanted was a family of my own, and I love you so damn much. There is nothing—and I mean, nothing—that could beat watching your belly swell with my baby growing inside of you."

She lets out a guttural cry. One filled with relief and joy.

"I love you so much," she mutters between sobs.

I stand, pick her up into my arms, and carry her down the hallway toward our bedroom.

I kick the door open and walk inside, and then we are all hands. She pulls my shirttail loose from my jeans as I guide us to the bed.

I set her down and unbutton the flannel. I shrug it off, pull the T-shirt over my head, and drop it on the floor. Then I peel my jeans off.

She leans back and watches the show.

Once I'm down to nothing, she scoots forward, and her mouth finds my chest as she runs her hands over my sides and around my back.

I let her explore my skin as my body reacts, and I grow hard between us.

When I can take no more, I reach under her arms and tug her up so I can turn us. I take a seat and pull her into my lap.

She starts to move her hips urgently as I strip her tee and bra.

She groans and throws her head back when I take one breast into my hand.

I love that sound. It's a deep, guttural reflex that lets me know what I'm doing feels good.

One second, my tongue is lapping at a taut pink nipple, and the next, she is pushing me to my back and crawling on top of me.

"What are you doing?" I ask breathlessly.

"You're taking too long," she growls as she bears up, slides her lounge pants down her long, sexy legs, and kicks them to the side.

Impatient girl.

I plant my feet, raise my hips, and circle them. My erection pressing into her silk panties.

"Oh, yes, sweet contact," she cries.

I don't think I've ever been this turned on before. My body is coiled tight and ready to pounce, but I keep my restraint and let her take control.

Her fingernails scrape their way down my abdomen, every muscle flexing as the burn of her touch lingers.

"You're so beautiful. I can't believe a part of you, of us, is growing inside of me," she whispers.

With that, I hook my arms around her waist and flip her to her back.

I lay a gentle kiss just below her belly button.

"I hope she looks just like you," I mutter against her skin.

"She?"

My eyes snap to hers.

"Just a hunch," I say.

I hook a finger into the hem of her panties and slowly slide them down her thighs.

Her legs fall open, totally exposing herself to me.

Complete trust. Complete surrender.

I want to take it slow, but I'm so damn ready, and so is my girl.

My finger glides through her wetness before I rise and my cock finds her entrance.

Finally.

I move inside her. Gently. Deeply.

We keep a slow-building pace. My eyes never leave hers until my control snaps and I can no longer hold back.

She locks her knees to my sides as my hips move urgently. She rises to meet my powerful thrusts as the burning sensation crawls up my spine.

I hold my breath and refuse to let go until her gasps turn ragged and I feel her muscles tighten around me.

I watch as she gives in to the sensation and cries my name as she comes.

Once her body calms, I enter her two more times, and an explosion of pleasure sweeps me up. She scores her nails down my back, and I cover her mouth with mine.

She drinks my muffled cries until we're both panting and sated.

Fuck, I love this woman.

I thought I'd known what those words meant before, but until Maxi came into my life, I was only experiencing an illusion of love.

This is real.

This is forever.

This is my family.

Chapter
six

Anna

THE SUN HANGS LOW IN THE SKY, CASTING LONG SHADOWS across the snow-covered front yard of the house Mike purchased for us all those years ago. It doesn't look like much. Just a modest but charming cottage.

We were so happy the day we moved in. Mike scooped me up into his arms and carried me over the threshold into our new life.

I stand here, clutching the old brass doorknob, feeling the weight of the past and the promise of the future pressing against my heart.

Weston asked us—me and my daughter, Kaela—to move in with him last night.

He made the case after dinner when I was gathering all of Kaela's things to pack into the diaper bag so we could head home.

For months now, we've been trekking across town to work and splitting our time between here and Weston's cabin. Toting a sleepy baby night after night.

All of our things are spread out, and Weston decided a few

weeks ago that he was going to outfit one of his spare bedrooms with furniture so Kaela would be comfortable in a crib instead of the pack 'n' play when we did stay the night.

"I hate when you leave. It's dark and snowy. Why don't you stay tonight?" he asked.

"We haven't been home in days. I need to go check on the house, collect the mail, and get new clothes for me and Kaela," I started rattling off.

"Why don't you two just move in here?"

I knew it was coming. It's the next natural step in our relationship, but it will be hard to say good-bye to this place.

Mike was a firefighter, a hero who fought fires with unwavering bravery. It was that job, battling raging flames that were devouring the mountainside and threatening homes, that took him from me. He made the ultimate sacrifice to protect Balsam Ridge, and he left behind a legacy of courage and a heart full of love for me and Kaela—our precious baby girl he never got to meet.

She toddles around the front porch, her tiny fingers reaching for the wet snow that has gathered on one of the rocking chairs.

She has inherited her father's bright blue eyes, infectious smile, and curious nature.

Every day as she grows, I see a new glimpse of Mike in her—a reminder of the love we shared.

I take a deep breath, the crisp scent of pine and wood burning filling my senses.

The memories of our first Christmas in this house flood back— our laughter as we decorated the tree he had cut down, the aroma of Mike's famous spaghetti sauce wafting through the kitchen, and the nights spent cuddled up by the fireplace, watching holiday movies together. It was our dream home, a place where we planned to spend many joy-filled Christmas mornings together as we watched our family grow.

But life has a way of forcing us to pivot and create new dreams.

It wasn't easy. The grief of losing the man I loved almost caused me to drown, but I had to push forward—for me and for Kaela.

Weston Tuttle was an unexpected blessing. He came along and helped me heal when I didn't think it was possible.

A sweet, funny, and gentle soul who slowly and patiently mended the cracks in my heart.

We had crossed paths at community events before, and his brother was Mike's boss and friend.

Our relationship started as a friendship, and when I began working for him last year, our connection grew stronger.

Love blossomed when I wasn't looking for it and least expected it, like a flower pushing through the ashes of the burned forest.

How lucky am I to have found it not once, but twice in a lifetime?

I hear a truck engine rumble to a stop and the sound of the door opening and closing.

Weston appears by my side, and he scoops Kaela into his arms.

His strong and calming hand rests on my shoulder, grounding me in the present.

His blue eyes, filled with understanding, meet mine, and I know that I'm not alone in facing the memories of this house.

"Hey, baby," he whispers. "Are you sure you're ready?"

I nod, my throat tight with a mixture of emotions. "Yes. It's time."

He hands Kaela to me and walks back down to his truck. He pulls a sign from the back and carries it to the curb.

He plants it in the snow by the freshly shoveled sidewalk.

Available for long-term lease. Tuttle and Sons Realty. Call today and ask for Jena.

I breathe a sigh of relief.

We discussed putting it on the market, but I just couldn't do it. Weston is the one who suggested that I use it as rental income until Kaela is older.

Then, I can sign it over to her, and she can decide to live in it or sell it.

My next-door neighbor, Brandee, appears on her porch.

"I don't like this in the least," she shouts.

"Jena promised to find someone nice to lease it to," Weston assures her.

"They'd better be nice and handsome and single," she says.

He chuckles. "I'll let her know."

Her eyes come to me, and she sticks her bottom lip out.

"Come over. I'll open a bottle of wine, and we can have a good cry," I say.

"Be there in thirty," she agrees.

Weston sprints back to us and opens the door. I step into the house, feeling the familiar creak of the wooden floor beneath my feet.

I set Kaela down, and her small feet pad softly toward a pile of toys tucked in the corner beside the sofa.

As I mentally began the process of packing, memories, both sweet and bitter, wash over me like a tidal wave. There, in the living room, is the spot where Mike told me our offer had been accepted. The keys tucked into his pocket, he fished them out and got down on one knee, asking me to be a homeowner with him.

Tears well up in my eyes as I recall the overwhelming joy I felt in that moment as he proudly presented them to me.

In the kitchen, I run my fingers over the countertop, where

Mike prepared countless meals for us. He was the chef in the family, always testing new recipes for the boys at the firehouse out on me.

His spaghetti sauce was legendary among our friends and neighbors.

Kaela chatters happily to her favorite stuffed bear, the one Weston got her for her first Valentine's Day.

I watch her squeal with delight as Weston takes the bear in his hands and starts talking back to her in a deep voice.

She's so happy. She loves Weston, and she doesn't understand the weight of the past or the significance of this move.

To her, it's all an adventure with her favorite humans.

I make my way to the bedroom. I open the closet and gaze at the singed uniform that still hangs there, neatly pressed and untouched since the hospital returned it to me. His scarred helmet rests on a shelf beside the wooden box containing the flag that covered his casket.

I take a deep breath, vowing to always honor his memory and the legacy he left behind.

I can hear his voice in my head loud and clear. *"It's okay, Anna. I'll always be with you, but it's okay to move forward."*

The doorbell rings, pulling me from my thoughts, and I walk back to the front of the house to find Brandee holding a bottle of champagne.

Weston builds us a fire in the fireplace.

I spread a blanket on the floor and sit with Kaela, her eyes growing heavy with sleep, as Brandee and Weston wrestle to pop the bottle in the kitchen.

The flames of the fire flicker, casting dancing shadows on the walls behind the sofa, and the house seems to sigh, as if it were letting go of us too.

"Anna," Brandee says softly as she joins me with two flutes, "I know today must be hard for you."

I take one of the glasses from her hand, and she takes a seat beside me on the floor.

I nod, unable to find the words to express the depth of my emotions.

"But it's also a new beginning," she continues, "and as salty as I am at Weston for stealing you from me, it's a chance for you guys to create new memories together."

I can feel the tears welling up in my eyes again, but this time, they aren't tears of sadness; they are tears of hope.

I lean over and rest my head on her shoulder. "I'm ready," I murmur.

"Glad one of us is," she grumbles.

Weston appears with his own flute of bubbly.

Brandee raises hers in the air. "To new beginnings," she bellows.

We clink our glasses together and shout the same.

Weston takes a sip, then sets it on the coffee table and reaches for Kaela. "Let me have her. I'll get her changed and read her a story while you two watch that sappy Christmas movie," he offers.

I hand my sleepy daughter off to him, and she instantly goes limp in his arms as he whispers to her.

Brandee and I watch as they disappear down the hallway.

"Dammit, there is nothing sexier than a man being sweet to a baby, is there?" Brandee mumbles.

"Nope," I agree.

"I'm so happy for you. I'd ask if he had a brother you could set me up with, but we all know that door has slammed shut," she gripes.

"I take it, your date didn't go well last night?" I ask.

She frowns. "He wore sunglasses. In the restaurant. I kept

waiting to see if he'd realize it. Like, *I can't see the menu that well. Why is it so dark in here? Oh, silly me. I forgot to take these off.* Or maybe they were those stupid transition lenses that are supposed to lighten up once you're out of the sunlight. But nope. He was just a douche-bag," she explains.

"Ew."

"Right? And that's not the worst part. His card was declined. I ended up paying for dinner and a taxi home because I wasn't getting back in the car with him."

I listen to her recount her experience and think to myself, *Some people go their whole lives searching for true love. Hoping to make an intimate connection with another human being. How blessed am I that I found it not once, but twice?*

"Sara-Beth did say the boys have some single cousins coming to the wedding," I tell her.

Her head snaps to me. "The hell you say?"

I nod.

"Interesting."

I laugh, and the heaviness of the day seems to float off my shoulders and away.

I look up to the ceiling and smile.

New beginnings.

Chapter
seven

Weston

I'M STANDING IN THE OFFICE, FACING DOWN AN ANGRY ANNA.

She has been spending most days at the boutique since the ski resort opened, and today was a busy day, as the Santa's Village—complete with holiday shopping, food, and the big guy himself—opened this morning. I offered to take Baby Duck to spend the day with me, as December is usually a slow month on the farm.

Stupid me forgot to bring the backpack baby carrier I'd purchased this morning, so when it was time for me and the farm manager, Rich, to take a hike out to one of the back fields to discuss some new planting in the greenhouse, I got creative.

"Oh my God, what did you do?" Anna cries as she takes in the sight.

"I needed to go down to the greenhouse, and I had a lot to carry, so I improvised."

"You improvised by duct-taping our daughter to you?" she squeals.

I look down at my chest, where Kaela is currently sleeping. I dressed her in her one-piece snowsuit and taped her up tightly. Facing out so she could see the beautiful mountainside as we hiked out to the location. She laughed and chattered the entire time.

Snug as a bug.

"I didn't duct-tape Baby Duck. Just her clothes. And look how strong the hold is," I explain as I fling my arms out to the sides and jump up and down.

Kaela doesn't even rouse.

"It's awesome, right?"

Anna's jaw drops, her voice a mixture of disbelief and outrage as she says, "You're kidding, right? You can't just tape our baby to yourself like some bizarre DIY project!"

Our baby.

It's the first time she's ever called Kaela ours, and the sound of it knocks me in the chest like a physical blow.

Anna doesn't realize the impact that one word has on me as she grabs a pair of scissors from the nearby desk and begins to carefully cut away the duct tape.

"Come on, Anna. You have to give me a little credit. It worked, and Kaela had a ball."

She finishes freeing Kaela from her duct-taped cocoon and cradles her in her arms.

Then, she looks at me, and her annoyance turns to amusement.

She begins to giggle, and before I know it, we are both laughing.

I walk over and wrap an arm around the two of them.

"I promise, no more duct-taped escapades with the baby," I say sheepishly.

"Thank you." She kisses the underside of my jaw as she cuddles Kaela.

"Ready to go tackle more packing?" I ask.

"Yeah, Langford loaded some boxes from the resort in the back of my car," she says.

I grin and grab the roll of duct tape from the conference table. "Perfect. I've got the tape."

Erin, Taeli, and Brandee showed up at the cottage to help Anna sort and box her and Kaela's things.

I toss some of the items they designated for donation in the back of my truck and head to the church in town to drop them off.

Once I deliver and help the pastor unload, I leave my truck parked and walk over to the cemetery on the hill across from the church.

I walk along the sidewalk that weaves into the beautifully land-scaped space. The ground is covered in freshly fallen snow and dotted with pops of color on the flower-covered marble memorials. Each one is a testament to a life lived and lost.

Finding the one gravestone I came to see, I stop and kneel to brush the snow aside and read the name.

"Hi, Mike," I whisper as I take in the stone that has both his and Anna's name carved in it.

The thought of losing her hits me out of nowhere, and my chest tightens with pain.

Minutes pass as I sit quietly, taking in the significance of this moment and arranging the words I want to say to him in my head.

Finally, I just speak my heart. "Ah shit. Look, man. We didn't know each other all that well, and I know that if you were given a choice, I'd probably be the last asshole on earth you'd have chosen to spend the rest of his life with your girls. I'll admit, I wasn't worthy. Hell, I'm still not worthy, but I love them, Mike. Anna doesn't know it yet, but I bought a ring. Two actually. One for her and one for Kaela. Because I know they come as a package deal. Love them both so much that I can't breathe when I imagine my life without the two of them in it. They make me a better man, and I swear on my life that I will do everything in my power to deserve their love and be that better man for them always. I'll protect them, make them laugh, chase off any little asshole like you and me that comes sniffing around Kaela, and most importantly, I'll love them as you would love them. I promise. You can trust them to me until you meet again. So, I guess I came here to ask your permission."

As I speak the last word, the wind rustles through the branches of the holly bushes that line the walkway nearby.

And then, as if in response to my plea, a flash of crimson catches my eye. A red cardinal lands on a branch, its brilliant feathers standing out against the green of the leaves.

It stares at me with a curious, almost-knowing gaze.

I smile at it, and it takes flight.

Cardinals have always been Mom's favorite bird—a symbol of hope and love, sent by our loved ones in heaven to watch over us.

It feels like a message, a silent approval from the man who once held Anna's heart.

"Thanks, man," I say through the lump in my throat.

I stand to make my way back to our girls, but stop and add one last thing. "Oh, and I did purchase the plot right over there. So, when the time comes, Anna will be between the two of us because I'm a good man, but not so good that I wouldn't be jealous if you got to have her laid to rest with just you for all eternity. Thank you again … for giving your life to save my home and for bringing those beautiful girls to Balsam Ridge. You'll always be my hero, man. Merry Christmas."

The entire ride back to the cottage, I plan how I'm going to ask Anna to marry me.

I don't want to overwhelm her. Her emotions have been all over the place as she said good-bye to the cottage, but I don't think I can wait. I purchased the rings weeks ago, wanting to propose on Christmas. Asking her to move in before wasn't part of the plan. It was a spontaneous reaction to having to send them off into the cold night again. So, screw plotting and trying to pick the perfect time and setting.

Spontaneous it is.

When I pull up to the cottage, my mother's car has joined the rest. I jump out and make my way into the warmth of the living room, where Mom is sitting with Leona, Kaela on her lap.

"Weston," she greets.

"Hi, Mom. Where's Anna?" I ask distractedly.

"Right here."

I turn to see her standing in the hallway. A box in her arms.

"Come here," I request.

She walks toward me, and I take the box from her and set it to the side.

"What's going on? Is something wrong?" she asks.

I clear my throat and reach into my pocket. Beads of sweat forming on my forehead.

She eyes me curiously as Erin, Taeli, and Brandee appear behind her.

I take a deep breath and sink to my knees.

Anna gasps, and Mom lets out a cry.

I open the box, where two diamond rings are nestled in velvet.

"Anna, I bought this ring a while ago because I've known for a long time that I want you to be my wife, and when I asked you to move in, the last thing I intended was for you to think I wanted to be roommates. I want to be a family. A committed family. You, me, and Baby Duck for as long as the good Lord allows us. Will you marry me and make me the happiest asshole in Tennessee?"

Her hand covers her mouth as she stares at the rings.

"Please," I plead.

"There are two," she murmurs.

Mom realizes what the moment is and sets Kaela on her feet. She waddles over to me, and I catch her in one arm.

I bring my eyes back to Anna.

"This one is for you," I say as I take her hand and place the emerald-cut diamond on her finger. "And this one is for you." I take the tiny band with its own smaller emerald-cut diamond and put it on Kaela's chubby finger. It nearly fits. "Because I'm asking both of you to have me for the rest of your lives."

Kaela coos and brings her hand to her mouth and begins to bite at the ring.

"That's a yes, isn't it, Baby Duck? Now, all we need is for Mommy to say yes too," I tell her.

We both look up to Anna.

She starts nodding frantically as tears stream down her cheeks. "Yes, yes, I will marry you, Weston Tuttle," she cries.

I scoop Kaela up and put her on my hip, and we stand. Anna throws her arms around my neck, and I draw her in for a long, deep kiss as my heart swells.

The girls start cheering, and Mom and Leona join us in celebration.

It wasn't the proposal I planned, but somehow, it's perfect.

"I'm calling everyone. We're going to have an engagement party tonight," Mom declares.

"It's already six. You can't get everyone together that quickly," Brandee says.

Erin laughs. "Sara-Beth and Leona Tilson can throw a party at the drop of a hat."

"It's perfect. Garrett just made it to town this afternoon. Weston's house at eight o'clock. You girls help spread the word. Let's go, Leona. We need to get to the market before it closes."

They grab their coats and run out of the door.

"I'm not so sure Garrett's going to think it's perfect timing since they just made it home," Erin mumbles.

"I'm sure he won't mind when he hears Weston's big news," Taeli says.

"Riiiiight," Brandee adds.

Anna glances around the room. "I guess the packing is done for now," she says.

I kiss her again.

"We have all the time in the world to move. Tonight, I just want to enjoy you," I say.

Chapter
eight

Sara-Beth

LEONA AND I HURRY TO GET EVERYTHING READY FOR THE evening. On the way to the market, we discuss the food. Since it's a celebration for Anna and Weston, we settle on sushi and pizza—their favorites. Well, sushi is Anna's favorite, and we don't have time to prepare Weston's favorite meal, so we compromise on pizza.

I place an order for the sushi, and we head into the market for supplies to make a fruit and veggie tray, along with a charcuterie board, and a couple bottles of champagne.

I text Ansley and ask that she bring a few sweet treats from the café. Then, I text Taeli to ask that she and Graham pick up wine.

Maxi and Corbin offer to stop by the florist and purchase flowers for Anna.

Langford calls to tell me that he let Zoey and Morris leave early, but he has to stay until the chairlifts close for the evening, and then he'll pick up Isley.

Tucker's mother came to town and picked Tucker up so they could visit her parents for the holidays before Garrett and Ansley's wedding.

"Ralph is going to get Hilton, and they'll stop at the pizzeria," Leona says as we load our purchases in the trunk.

We pop into the restaurant once we receive the text that our order is ready, and then we head straight to Weston's cabin.

"I can't believe Weston proposed and we happened to be there to witness it," Leona says.

"I know," I agree.

He is the one son that I worried would never settle down. Now, here he is, about to become a husband and stepfather. Just goes to show you that your children can surprise even you.

We get everything set up as quickly as possible. Leona makes a pitcher of sweet tea and a pitcher of lemonade while I pull platters down to hold the sushi.

We spread it out buffet-style across the kitchen island, along with the trays and meat and cheese board.

Morris returns with the bag of ice we asked him to bring and fills the standing cooler by the deck door, where we set up a beverage station.

Everyone begins to trickle in and make plates.

Anna and Weston first.

"Well, this is certainly different than our usual party meals," Graham says as he looks over the buffet of sushi rolls.

I shrug. "It's Anna's favorite, and this celebration is for her. Plus, it was easy. We just called it all into the new Japanese restaurant in the valley, and they had it ready in no time," I say.

"I hope you guys have something else to serve other than sushi because Isley's been getting so hangry lately," Taeli muses.

"Isley loves sushi," Brandee states.

"I know, but she can't eat it while she's pregnant," Taeli explains.

"Oh, right."

Maxi, who is standing across the island with a plate loaded with food, spits out the piece of sashimi she was chewing.

"Are you okay?" Taeli asks.

"Why can't she eat it?" she asks.

Taeli eyes her suspiciously. "Isley? Because it's raw. It's dangerous to eat raw fish while pregnant," Taeli explains.

"Oh," Maxi says as she sets her plate to the side. Her hand goes to her stomach as her face turns green.

"Maxi, are you …" Taeli asks.

She nods.

"Oh my goodness," I shriek as the joy of hearing I'm expecting another grandchild hits me.

I walk quickly to her and take her face in my hands.

"Oh, Maxi, congratulations," I whisper through tears.

She sniffles. "I'm going to be terrible at this."

"No, you're not. You're going to be a kick-ass mother," I correct.

She shakes her head.

"Yes, you will," Anna says.

She looks at Anna. "Why would you think that?"

"Well, um, you babysit Kaela, and you're great with her," Anna notes.

"That's because she's easy and she's a baby. Eventually, she'll get bigger and mouthy and sneaky and shit."

"Oh God, I hope not!" Anna cries.

I laugh. "Oh, she will. Kids do that," I quip.

"Yeah, or they get arrested for stealing a patrol car their senior year and almost lose their scholarship," Leona says.

She passes me a glass of wine, and I take it as I laugh.

"Or sneak out and run away to Nashville in the middle of the night with an underage girl in tow," I state.

"Or leave school and the scholarship they and you worked so hard to secure, only to marry a dumbass and move across the country," Leona continues.

"Or get married young and widowed young," I add.

"Or run off on you after their father dies and leave you to run a farm alone," Leona muses.

"Or get divorced and end up the single father of a baby boy, or come home one day to tell you they're going to be a pot farmer, or you pick up a newspaper to read they got a DUI and are being accused of having an illegitimate child," I conclude.

I swallow the entire glass of wine, and Leona passes me the bottle.

All their eyes come to me.

"Not to worry though. It's all worth it in the end. I mean, look around this room, and you'll see the reward that you reap."

"Plus, you all have to take care of us when we get old and senile and streak down Main Street if we get a wild hair," Leona quips.

Maxi sits down on one of the barstools.

"Not sure you two are helping," Anna says as she fetches Maxi a glass of tea.

"Don't worry; Hilton and Ralph will be here with pizza any minute," Leona tells Maxi.

Erin and Ted walk in, and she looks around the room.

"What'd I miss?"

We fill her in and then Isley when she and Langford finally arrive, and the party turns into a celebration of both Weston and Anna's and Corbin and Maxi's big news.

Hilton finds me leaning on the threshold of the kitchen, watching them all enjoy the food and each other's company.

He clasps my shoulders from behind and kisses the top of my head. "How are you holding up, my darling?" he asks.

I reach up and place my hand over one of his. "Look at them. They're all so happy, and that makes me the happiest mother in the world," I answer.

Garrett catches sight of us, and he elbows Langford. They walk over to join us, their brothers following them.

"What are you two over here whispering about?" Garrett asks.

"We're just proud of you boys—that's all," I say.

"I'm the favorite though, right, Mom?" Weston asks.

I shake my head. "I never said that."

"It's okay. They already know it's true; you can admit it," he encourages.

"No way. I was the firstborn. I made her a mother," Langford cuts him off.

"Yeah, well, I'm the one who wrote a song for her and sang it on the Grammys in front of the entire world," Garrett brags.

Morris pushes through them. "I'm the baby. Everyone knows the baby is always the favorite." He kisses my cheek.

"You aren't even second or third, runt," Corbin quips. "I save lives. Just sayin'."

"Well, I'm the handsome one. She could never resist this smile and my dimple," Weston declares.

"We all have the same dimple, dumbass," Langford points out.

Graham just shakes his head and doesn't say a word.

"What about Graham?" Garrett asks.

"Psst, he's Pop's favorite. He can't have Mom too," Weston gripes.

All their eyes go to Hilton.

"All I wanted was a dog. If your momma wasn't so damn irresistible, I'd have half a dozen bluetick hounds to take out hunting on the weekends instead of you knuckleheads."

"That's not true, is it, Mom?" Morris asks.

"Oh, Hilton, stop teasing the boys," I say. Then, I mouth to them, *You're welcome*. And wink.

"Eww, God, Mom," Weston whines.

They scurry off.

Langford pulls Hilton aside, and I stand at the edge of the room, a proud smile gracing my lips as I watch my six adult sons tease each other. They all remind me of their father in different ways.

They've grown into strong, capable men, and moments like this fill my heart with immense pride, as I'm secure in the knowledge that they will always have each other's backs. They're a living, breathing testament to the values we tried to instill in them—the importance of family, loyalty, and unwavering support.

I know they will continue that legacy with their own children.

And that's the goal of every mother—to leave this world knowing you left it a little better than you found it and know that you will live on in the generations that come after you.

"Come on, Mom. It's time to open the champagne."

Graham's voice pulls me from my thoughts.

I shift my gaze to him, and he stands with his elbow out for me to take.

I wrap my arm around his and let him guide me to the back deck, where the girls are already passing out glasses.

Garrett pops the cork and starts to pour as Langford taps on the edge of his flute to get everyone's attention.

"A toast to my brother Weston. Congratulations for finding a woman crazy enough to hitch her wagon to yours. And to my brother Corbin. Welcome to the scary world of fatherhood."

"Hear, hear!" Hilton shouts as we all raise our glasses and drink.

Chapter
nine

Langford

MY PHONE DINGS, AND I FISH IT FROM MY BACK POCKET.

The package is en route.

I look at my watch and see it's half past ten and go in search of my bride. I find her on the couch in deep conversation with Maxi.

"Hey, beautiful. Are you ready to go?"

She yawns, and I chuckle.

"I'll take that as a yes."

She smiles and looks at Maxi. "That's another side effect. You'll start being tired all the time."

"Yep, already there," Maxi confirms.

Isley places a hand on her knee. "It'll all be worth it. Just call me whenever you have questions and don't buy any clothes. I have maternity clothes in every size from first preggo to about to pop. I'll have Langford bring you a tote tomorrow from my first trimester."

"Thanks, Isley."

I don't know what all they've talked about for the last hour and a half, but Maxi looks a hundred times more relaxed than she did when we arrived.

Offering her my hand, I help Isley to her feet.

"I'll go grab my coat from the mudroom," she says.

Mom finds me waiting by the front door, carrying a pizza box. "Here, take this with you. It's the one with pineapple on it. Isley's the only one who'll eat it," she says.

I take the box from her hand. "Are you okay here?" I ask.

"Yes, your father texted me from the road. I'm going to stay here, and Leona and I'll clean up, and she'll drop me off on her way home. You go and have a great night."

I kiss her cheek, and Isley appears.

"Oh, is that pineapple pizza?" she asks.

"I thought you and the baby might want a midnight snack," Mom says as she hugs my wife.

"I think she wants a snack for the ride home," Isley says.

I guide her carefully across the snow-covered lawn to my truck that is parked at the top of the drive.

She enjoys her pizza while I drive us home.

Isley curls up in the living room, her hand resting gently on her growing belly. Her eyes are on the twinkling Christmas tree we decorated before Tucker left with his mother.

It's our first Christmas as a family, and this house has never felt more like a home.

I join her with a cup of hot cocoa.

"Thank you," she says as she leans into my side.

I wrap an arm around her and tug her in close.

"It's so quiet here without Tuck. I don't like it," she says.

I kiss her forehead. "He'll be back soon."

She sighs. "I know. I just miss him."

"Me too."

She lifts her head and raises an eyebrow. "But we do have the house to ourselves. Might be the last time for a long while. Wanna make love by the light of the Christmas tree?"

Fuck me.

"I thought you were tired?"

She smiles, and her tongue darts out and licks at my neck just below my earlobe.

"I can rally," she whispers.

My cock grows hard at the contact and the words from her sweet mouth, and I groan.

Her hand travels down my chest toward the zipper on my jeans, and I place mine on it to halt her progress.

She jerks back in surprise. "What's wrong?" she asks.

"Um, I have a headache," I rattle off the lie.

"A headache? Really?" she scoffs.

"Yep, a pounding one. Started on the way home. It's killing me."

Her frustration turns to concern as she brings the back of her hand to my forehead.

"No fever. You've been working too hard since the resort opened. Your body is probably trying to tell you to slow down," she says.

She's right. I've been working twelve-hour, sometimes fourteen-hour days since Thanksgiving.

I take her hand in mine. "I'm sorry, baby. It's been hectic with it being our first season, but I promise I'll slow down. I'm planning to have Morris trained to take on more responsibility before the baby comes so I can be here for you two."

She smiles. "That's great news. I think he'll do well."

"So do I."

Headlights flash across the window as we hear the rumble of an engine.

Isley's brows furrow. "Who could that be at this hour?"

I stand. "I'll go see."

I walk to the front door just as the four people pile out of the truck. I can feel Isley come up behind me and peek around my shoulder.

"Mom! Daddy!" Isley exclaims.

"Surprise, sweetheart. I thought it'd be nice to have your parents here for our first Christmas," I say as I turn to the side.

She hurries past me and down the front steps, her eyes welling up with tears of joy, and I follow.

Her mother, Evelyn, catches her in a tight embrace.

"How are you here?" Isley asks.

"Langford made all the arrangements. He bought the tickets for the three of us and sent a car to pick us up at your brother's house and take us to the airport in Pheonix and his father was waiting when we landed in Knoxville and drove us here," her mom explains.

"The three of you?"

"Yes, let me introduce you to Ezra. He is your father's nurse. He comes out to help us twice a week, but Langford thought that it might be easier on your father, on both of us, to have Ezra travel with us."

Isley and I shake the jovial gentleman's hand, and I thank him for being willing to spend the holiday away from his family to be with ours.

"It's my pleasure. I'll have many more years to spend with them, God willing. It's important for Mr. and Mrs. Paysour to have this time with their family. Besides, I was promised time on the slopes," Ezra says.

"All the time you want."

Isley's father looks around in confusion.

"Asa, aren't you going to say hello to Isley and Langford?" Evelyn asks him.

"Where's my briefcase?" he asks.

"We didn't bring your briefcase," she tells him.

"Yes, we did. I just had it."

Ezra moves to his side. "Mr. Paysour, it's my fault. I forgot it."

Asa frowns. "But I'll need it for my meeting."

"Don't you worry. I'll send for it in time for your meeting," Ezra says.

"Oh, okay, then," Asa mumbles.

Ezra guides his attention to us. "Look who's here. Do you know these guys?" Ezra asks him.

"Isley!" Asa bellows and opens his arms wide.

She steps into them.

He hugs her a moment and then releases her and looks down between them.

"Isley, you're going to have a baby," he says in wonder.

"I sure am. A girl," Isley chokes out.

"A girl. Did you hear that, Evelyn? A granddaughter. Isn't that wonderful?"

"Absolutely."

Asa places his hand on her bump and stares at it with tear-filled eyes. Then, he looks up at her. "You're gonna be a great mother."

"You think so, Daddy?"

"I know so."

She hugs him again, and then he looks over her shoulder to me.

"We gonna stand out in the cold all night, or are you gonna invite us in?"

I chuckle. "Follow me, sir."

Pop and Ezra unload the bags from the back of the truck and follow us to the door.

I open and hold it for them to enter, and as Isley slides by me, I whisper in her ear, "I'm getting a rain check on that sexy time by the Christmas tree, right?"

She grins up at me. "Oh, yeah. Definitely."

Thank God.

Chapter
ten

Isley

EZRA AND I GET MY PARENTS SETTLED INTO THE GUEST ROOM while Langford walks his father outside.

"Asa, do you have everything you need?" Ezra asks as Daddy climbs into bed.

"My reading glasses?"

"They're beside you on the nightstand, and the book you've been reading is beside them."

"Water?"

"I'll bring you a glass, Daddy," I offer.

"Did I take my meds?" he asks.

"Yes, sir. Before you brushed your teeth. You're good till the morning," Ezra says.

"Okay. Good night," Daddy says.

Mom crawls in with him and turns on the lamp, and then she curls on her side as he grabs the copy of *Wuthering Heights*, turns to the marked page, and starts to read aloud to her.

I mouth, *Good night*, to my mother and follow Ezra out into the hallway.

"He should be good for the night. I'll be back in the morning to help him shower and dress."

"You aren't staying here?" I ask.

"No, ma'am. Your husband has booked me in a deluxe suite at his hotel. I'm going to go order room service and soak in the hot tub," he says.

"You do that," I encourage.

He smiles and heads to the door.

"Ezra," I call after him.

He turns back to me.

"Do you have to bathe and dress him every day now?" I ask.

He shakes his head. "No, your mother and brother help him with everyday tasks. I'm mostly there a few days a week to sort his medications and assess him to keep a record of his progression."

"Okay."

"He's still doing well. He has days where he's completely lucid."

I nod. "Thank you again for flying with them."

"You have a good night. I'll be back in the morning."

He walks out, and I watch out the window as Langford talks to him and Hilton before shaking Ezra's hand.

My heart swells with gratitude for my thoughtful husband. He knows how much my parents mean to me, especially my daddy, who is suffering from early-onset Alzheimer's disease.

I keep in contact with them and try to FaceTime and call at least once a day, but the disease has been progressing, and sometimes, he doesn't even recognize my voice. It's like he's talking to a stranger, and it's scary. I know it has to be terrifying for my mother.

Every moment with him is precious.

Hilton's truck roars to life, and when Langford returns inside, I run to him.

Burying my face in his chest, I begin to sob.

He holds me close and lets me get it all out. Then, he picks me up off my feet and carries me to our bedroom.

"I need to take Daddy a glass of water," I mumble.

He sets me on the bed. "I'll get it. I want to say good night anyway."

I slip out of my leggings and sweater and pull on a maternity nightgown.

When he returns, he pulls off his clothes, and we climb into bed. I curl into his side as he clicks on the television mounted above the chest of drawers.

"Thank you so much for making this happen. I honestly didn't think it was a possibility," I tell him.

"I can't believe I was able to surprise you," he says.

"I should have known something was up when you gave me that bogus headache excuse," I quip.

"Yeah, I panicked. My dick was hard as a rock, and our parents were about to pull in."

I giggle.

"Do you have a headache now?" I ask.

He quirks an eyebrow. "You aren't suggesting we get naked with your parents down the hall, are you, Isley Tuttle?"

I slide my hand down to the band of his boxers.

"There are things we can do quietly," I suggest.

He grabs the remote from the nightstand and turns the volume up a few decibels, and I proceed to thank him properly.

The next morning, Langford picks Ezra up, and he comes to help Daddy get ready while I make breakfast. We plan to take them to the resort and show them around Santa's Village while Morris takes Ezra out for a day of skiing.

I make Daddy's favorite—pancakes and link sausages.

He eats two helpings, and then we all pile into Langford's truck.

"I forgot how beautiful the mountains are in the winter," Mom muses.

"Dang snow. I'll need to shovel our driveway when we get home," Daddy says.

Mom's eyes meet mine, and she shakes her head slightly.

Ezra talked to me and Langford this morning. He said that Daddy slips in between the past and present sometimes, and it's best not to contradict him. Pointing out that he is forgetting things or making things up in his head only leads to unnecessary agitation and fear on Daddy's part. So, when possible, we just go along with what he is experiencing at the time.

It's hard at first, but as the day progresses, it gets easier.

Mom and Ezra handle it all with ease, and if Mom can do it without breaking down and getting upset, so can I. I blame the few moments I walk away to compose myself on pregnancy hormones.

Langford, for his part, does everything he can to pack the day with holiday cheer.

"I want you to make a ton of Christmas memories," he tells me as we watch the carolers dressed in Dickens-era attire.

As I watch Daddy struggle to remember the words to familiar carols, my heart aches. But seeing Langford's unwavering support and love as he sits with him so Mom and I can peruse the shoppers gives me hope.

In this moment, I realize that the true magic of Christmas is not in the gifts or the decorations, but in the love and togetherness of a family.

"Let's take a picture with Santa," Mom suggests.

"Aren't we a little old to sit on the big guy's lap?" I tease.

"Santa is for everyone," she says as she grabs my hand.

We get into the line, and an elf hands us each a candy cane before we climb the steps to Santa's chair.

"I can't believe you want to do this. It's so not like you," I say.

She shrugs. "You're right; I used to be so reserved. I wish we had done more things like this when you were growing up."

"What changed?" I ask.

"We got that letter. Results of your father's test. It's easy to let go of all the nonsense when your time together is given an expiration date," she explains.

"Yeah, I bet."

She takes my hand and squeezes. "Promise me that you won't ever have to get a letter from a doctor to remember what's important."

"I promise."

Santa, who looks suspiciously like Mayor Gentry, waves us over, and Mom whispers her Christmas wishes in his ear too quietly for me to hear.

Then, it's my turn.

"I already have everything I could ever want, Santa, so I guess if I were to ask for anything, it would be a healthy baby," I say.

The photographer draws our attention, and Santa wraps his arm around the two of us.

They snap a Polaroid picture and hand it to me.

"Oh, can we get one more with our husbands?" I ask.

We wave Langford and Daddy over, and they stand side by side over Santa's shoulders.

"Everyone say, *Ho, ho, ho. Merry Christmas*," Santa prompts.

We do as instructed, and the photog snaps another photo. I shake them as the film develops.

I'll treasure them forever.

As the day draws to a close, Ezra rejoins us and recounts his exciting day, learning tricks from Morris and Zoey over dinner.

I can see that the event-filled day is taking its toll on Daddy as he struggles with his plate.

I fake a yawn. "Oh, wow. I'm super tired. I hate to be a party pooper, but this baby sure wears me out. Do you guys mind if we head home instead of going on the horse carriage ride tonight?"

"Sure. We can always do the ride tomorrow night," Langford assures.

He pays the check, and I hold on to my father's hand as we head to the truck.

"I love you, Daddy," I whisper.

He looks at me, a hint of recognition in his eyes, and manages a weak but loving smile as he squeezes my hand.

It was a great day. One I'll never forget. A day when my husband's thoughtful surprise brought my family closer together and gave us a Christmas to remember, even in the face of Alzheimer's disease.

Chapter
eleven

Morris

I WAKE UP ALONE. ZOEY'S SIDE OF THE BED IS STILL WARM.

The smell of coffee wafts through the air.

And I sit up, blinking against the early morning sunlight that is beaming through the window against the far wall.

I grab my phone from the nightstand and check the time.

We're supposed to shoot an advertising campaign for Misty Mountain Ranch and Ski Area today.

Garrett purchased some television ad space, a couple of road-side billboards in Tennessee and North Carolina, and print space in several travel magazines.

Garrett and Langford did an interview and had their photos taken at the resort yesterday, but today is all about the ski slopes.

Now that word is out that world-champion skier Zoey Phillips is working as an instructor at Misty Mountain, my brothers asked if she'd be willing to be a part of the marketing for the resort.

She was apprehensive at first.

With the charges filed against her former coach and the looming trial, she was afraid it could bring negative attention, but Langford assured her that he and Garrett didn't give a damn what people thought about what had happened during the investigation into the charges leveled against Taut. They are proud to have her image represent the resort.

I stand and go in search of Zoey and coffee when I hear the water running.

I follow the sound to the bathroom at the end of the hall. I open the door and can barely make out her naked form through the steam. The sexy sound of her voice singing a Taylor Swift song greets me.

I pull the T-shirt over my head and drop the pajama pants to the floor as I make my way to join her.

The glass is foggy, but I can see her standing under the spray, washing her hair.

I open the door and slide in behind her. She lets out a yelp of surprise as I run my hands down her slick, soapy sides.

"You scared me," she squeals as she relaxes against me.

"Sorry," I whisper into her ear.

"I was getting worried you weren't going to wake up and we would be late," she says.

"You should have awakened me before you got out of bed," I say.

She laughs. "Then, we definitely would have been late," she says as she glances over her shoulder at me.

I kiss the base of her neck, and she moans.

"Don't. We don't have time."

"I'm just here to share the shower and save time," I promise her, even as my growing erection presses into her.

"Morris," she gasps as her hand snakes around and strokes me.

I growl as I walk her to the back of the small shower and press her against the tiles.

She ducks under my arm and turns to face me. "I'm serious."

"You started it, sweetheart," I say as I fist my hand in her wet hair.

"You're the one who raided my shower," she points out.

"Right," I say before I take her mouth with mine.

Her hands come to my shoulders, and she rises on her toes to meet my lips. Her breasts graze my chest, and I tear my mouth from hers to lick a trail down to one rosy bud and take it between my teeth.

She jumps in my arms as I bite down, and my tongue darts out to soothe the peak before I suck it into my mouth again. I give her other breast the same attention before she grabs a handful of my hair and pulls me up and back to a kiss.

I walk her backward out of the water spray and against the shower wall. She looks up at me, a teasing look in her eye as she bites my bottom lip. Then, she takes my cock into her hand and begins to slowly, torturously pump my flesh.

I plant my hands above her and lean my forehead against the cool tiles above her head.

She slides to her knees, and I have to brace myself as she wraps her lips around the head of my throbbing erection and leisurely sucks it into her mouth. Her eyes never leave mine as she takes me deeper.

Damn, this woman owns me.

I groan as her teeth graze the sensitive skin and her hands whip me into a frenzy.

"Fuck, I love you," I manage to murmur as the rhythm of her hands and mouth working together bring me to the brink.

I close my eyes and let the sensation rocket down my spine and draw my balls tight.

"Zoey, I'm going to come, baby," I warn.

She quickens her pace, taking me to the back of her throat, and I try to hold on. Not wanting this to end, but I can't control it.

I roar her name as my seed floods her mouth. She stays on her knees until I'm completely spent and she's milked every drop from me.

When she stands, I reach and pull her to me and kiss her deeply.

"You drive me crazy," I rasp as I kiss her cheeks, her eyes, her nose.

"The feeling is mutual," she says.

She turns and steps back into the spray.

I grasp her waist. "Where do you think you're going?"

"I'm finishing my shower so we can go," she exclaims.

I pull her hips forward and use my knee to spread her legs.

"Morris, we don't have time," she cries.

But as soon as my fingers slide between her legs, her words of protest die on her lips, and she throws her head back against me.

I pinch her clit, and her body begins to tremble.

"That's my girl, always ready for me," I say as I sink my teeth into her earlobe.

I find her opening hot and slick and start pumping one finger in and out. I curl it inside her and find that spot that I know drives her wild.

Her muscles start to spasm, and I know she's close.

"Oh, yes, right there," she mutters.

I add another finger and bring my thumb up to apply pressure and run circles around her clit.

Her arms shoot out to the sides, and she braces herself as she rides my hand while her body quakes.

I hold her tight to my chest as her orgasm explodes. When the last tremble rocks through her, she goes limp against me.

I wait until her breathing evens out to let go of her and take hold of the bottle of body wash perched on the built-in shelf.

I pour some into my hand and begin to run both of them over her until she is covered in a sweet-smelling lather. While she rinses, I quickly wash my hair and body.

Once we're both clean, she turns off the flow while I fetch two towels.

"We're going to be so late," she says as she wraps her long, wet locks.

I grin at her. "Totally worth it."

She shakes her head and pushes me out of the bathroom. "Go away. I have to do my hair and makeup, and I don't need any more distractions."

I leave her to it and go to pour us a cup of coffee.

We're going to need the energy.

Chapter
twelve

Zoey

I STAND HERE AT THE BOTTOM OF THE SLOPE, THE CRISP mountain air at my back and the snow crunching softly beneath my boots, and wait for Morris to join me. The early winter sun casts a warm, golden glow over the Smoky Mountains, and we honestly couldn't have asked for a more breathtaking backdrop for today's photo shoot.

Langford and the photographer, Erica, are talking over the images he wants her to capture as I bend to strap into my skis.

"Wait, Zoey. I want to get a few snaps of you holding your skis under the Misty Mountain Ranch and Ski Area sign," Erica calls.

I'm itching to get on the mountain, but I oblige and make my way over to the wooden sign that stands above the entrance to the chairlifts.

Morris exits the locker room and joins us.

He looks amazing. Langford and Garrett had cool retro

snowsuits made for us. Mine is a teal one-piece suit with a white faux fur trim collar. His is red with brown fur.

The wording and resort logo on our skis match the suits.

"You guys look amazing," Garrett praises.

Morris starts striking silly poses.

I groan. "If you make me look bad, I'm going to kill you."

He throws an arm over my shoulders. "It's impossible to make you look bad," he murmurs.

"Okay, lovebirds, I'm liking this energy. Let's get some of your chemistry on camera while we still have this great natural light. Then, we'll switch it up, and I'll get video footage of the two of you playing around and racing on skis," Erica requests.

We spend the next two hours taking directions from Erica and her team.

Langford has poured his heart and soul into creating this ski resort, and I'm proud to be part of it.

Misty Mountain Ranch and Ski Area are about to become a sought-after winter travel destination, nestled deep in the heart of the Smokies.

The inaugural season has been a moderate success, due mainly to all of Langford's hands-on attention to detail, but with Garrett's star power and me lending my notoriety in the sports world as well as bringing my future training camp to Balsam Ridge, next year will be phenomenal.

"Zoey, you ready?"

Morris's voice pulls me from my thoughts.

I can't help but smile, my heart skipping a beat at the sight of him poised to ski the figure eight with me.

"Ready when you are, handsome," I call.

Erica gives us the signal to begin, and he takes my hand in

his and kisses my wrist before we glide down the mountainside together, our skis cutting graceful arcs in the freshly fallen snow. It's like a dance; we move in perfect synchronization.

As we descend, Erica captures the magic of the moment in every shot—our laughter, our shared glances, and the pure exhilaration of skiing in these majestic mountains. I know these photos and videos will be more than just promotional material; they will be memories frozen in time, reminding us of this precious period in our lives. Falling in love on the slopes.

At the bottom of the mountain, we stop to catch our breath.

Morris turns to me. "This place is incredible. I can't wait to see what it becomes."

I couldn't agree more.

It's not just a business; it's a testament to family, love, and the beautiful spirit of the Smoky Mountains.

"I think we have everything we need," Erica says as she watches the playback. "The camera loves you two."

Morris looks to Langford. "It's nice to know if this resort gig doesn't work out, I can always fall back on a modeling career."

Langford barks out a laugh. "You're lucky Zoey made you look good, brother. You'd better hope I don't fire your ass."

"Don't worry. I've got money," I tell him.

His eyes snap to me. "You do, huh?"

"Yeah, I really do," I say.

"How much are we talking?"

I shrug. "Like a whole lot. All those years of winning competitions and sponsorship bonuses and endorsement deals—I saved all of it."

His eyes go wide. "Are you telling me I got myself a sugar momma?"

"Yep, and you'd better hope I don't fire your ass," I tease.

Ansley's mother is hosting a bridal tea for her, so I have to quickly change, and Morris drops me off at Chantilly's Tea Room.

It's an old Victorian house, hugging the mountainside, that has been converted into a quaint event venue and boutique, filled with antique teapots and teacups and silver platters that hold finger sandwiches and bite-sized confections.

Today is the Wednesday before Christmas, and her wedding is in four days, so it's a complete surprise when she asks me to be a part of the bridal party for her and Garrett's wedding.

"Will you do us the honor of being our greeter?"

"What does a greeter do exactly?" I ask.

"You'll stand in the foyer and welcome the people as they arrive and direct them to sign the guest book before one of the groomsmen escorts them to their seats. I know it's not a glamorous job, but you and Morris didn't make it official in enough time for me to have a bridesmaid dress made for you," she begins to explain.

"Ansley, it's not going to hurt my feelings to simply be a guest at your wedding," I assure her.

"I know, but you're family now, and I want you to be a part of my big day."

I can hear the sincerity in her words.

I reach across the table and take her hand. "Then, I'd be honored to be your guest book person," I accept.

She smiles huge. "Thank you. I had the boutique send over a couple of dresses they had in stock in your size that match the color scheme. Garrett put the box in your office this morning, along with a gift from us. Pick whichever dress you like best."

Isley breezes in just as the tea is served. "Sorry I'm late. The live nativity at town hall got out of hand somehow. There are camels loose on Main Street. Wise men and shepherds in leather sandals chasing them on foot. It's complete mayhem."

"Aren't Tucker and Caleb playing shepherds this year?" Sara-Beth asks.

"Yep, they're having the time of their lives, trying to wrangle those beasts."

"Have mercy."

"I hope this isn't an omen for how the rest of the week is going to go," Ansley says.

"Don't worry. If any animals get loose at your wedding, your greeter will handle it," I assure her.

She looks at me and then bursts out laughing. Which causes us all to join her.

"No wedding day goes perfectly. There will be something that goes awry. You just have to let it all roll off your back and pivot in the moment. The only thing that matters is, at the end of the day, you are dancing with your new husband," Leona states.

"Yeah, but not every wedding is being broadcast to the world," Ansley mumbles.

"Hey, you listen to me. You forget those cameras are there. I know that becoming Mrs. Garrett Tuttle comes with some inconveniences, but I won't let it stress you out so much that you don't enjoy every second of your wedding day. I'll wrangle those magazine people myself and toss them out on their asses," Erin declares.

"I'll help. I have experience with tossing photographers on their asses," I volunteer.

"Thanks, you guys. You're all right. I'm letting the thought of them drive me insane. That stops now. I don't care what they capture or what they think. I'm going to relish every single minute."

"That's our girl," Erin bellows.

Chapter
thirteen

I PACE IN FRONT OF THE GIRLS, WHO ARE SEATED AT TWO TABLES in front of me.

I called a bridal party meeting in the reception hall ahead of tonight's rehearsal.

"Sara-Beth has given us a job, ladies. Tonight, we are all staying in adjoining rooms across the resort from the boys. Our mission, should we choose to accept it, is to keep Garrett Tuttle from sneaking a peek or copping a feel the night before the wedding. Are we all in?" I ask.

Maxi raises her hand.

"Yes?"

"Um, why do we have to spend the night away from our guys? We aren't getting married."

"Because Garrett Tuttle is a crafty devil and it will take every one of us standing guard. And we just thought it'd be fun for us all to spend the night together," I admit.

Maxi groans. "I see you bitches all the time. Corbin just worked a double shift so he could be off for the wedding and Christmas, my hormones are raging, and I wanted to make use of that big ole jetted tub and fancy king-size bed."

I cross my arms over my chest. "Fine. If you want to let the OGGs down, go right ahead."

Maxi's eyes dart to Sara-Beth, who is fussing over the table settings.

She huffs out a frustrated breath. "I'll stay with you guys."

That's what I thought.

"Does anyone else have a complaint?" I ask, scanning the room.

Silence.

"Nobody? So, we're all in?"

They nod.

"Excellent!"

I bring my eyes back to Maxi. "Sara-Beth said Garrett rented out the entire resort for four days, so you can still molest your fireman in the fancy hotel room," I inform her.

"Yes!"

Taeli raises her hand and then speaks. "What are we gonna do to celebrate Ansley's last night as a single lady?"

"I vote ice-skating!" Anna chimes.

"Oh, let's night ski. No one will be on the slopes. We'll have them all to ourselves," Zoey suggests.

"We could get drunk and go snow tubing," Brandee adds.

Ansley clears her throat, and our attention snaps to her.

"Can we do something, anything, that doesn't include the possibility of me or any of my bridesmaids breaking a leg or throwing up on the altar tomorrow? Please," she pleads.

"That's smart," Jena quips.

"We could take over the Cantina, and those of us who can hold our liquor can do shots and sing karaoke," I propose.

"Yeah, maybe we should stay in and drink one, maybe two bottles of wine," Brandee says.

"We could play board games," Taeli recommends.

"Oh, I know. How about a Christmas movie marathon? We can put on comfy clothes, pop some popcorn, and just veg out," Anna offers her input.

Ansley's hand shoots up. "I like that idea. I vote for movie night."

I roll my eyes. "Boring, but it is your night, so we'll do what you want to do."

"Thanks, I guess," Ansley mutters.

"Now that that's settled, everyone, go to your rooms and get your provisions for the night and meet back here. We'll all go to the rehearsal and dinner together and say our good-byes to the boys," I command.

"Who made her the boss of us?" Isley asks Jena.

"Ansley did when she made her maid of honor. The power has gone to her head," Jena replies.

"Come on, girls. Get a move on," I prompt.

Maxi stands and gives me a salute. "Aye, aye, Captain."

The rehearsal goes off without a hitch. Well, one hitch.

I thought Sara-Beth was going to have a heart attack when the pastor asked if anyone had any objections and one of Garrett's dumbass bandmates stood up and yelled, "What about me?"

Wish I had thought to do that.

Dinner is served immediately afterward, and once the dessert is finished, I snapped my fingers, and all the girls stand up.

"Kiss your guys good night, ladies," I demand.

We all say our good-byes and leave them sitting around the tables, drinking whiskey.

I'm the last one in line as I follow the others out the door, and I pause and turn back to the room of men.

"One more glass apiece, and then you'd better all go to bed," I warn.

They grin.

They're not going to go to bed.

I can't worry about them. Graham will have to fight that battle. My job tonight is to keep Ansley's mind occupied and her mind off *Country Daily*.

We all pile into her suite and change into our matching silk pajamas.

"Should we wait and put these on in the morning? What if we spill wine on them or popcorn butter?" Brandee asks.

"Shh," I shush her.

"There will be no talk of accidents or spills or anything at all negative tonight. We're all going to be adults and use napkins and carefully sip our drinks. Got it?" I whisper so Ansley doesn't hear me.

"Got it," they all agree.

There is a knock at the door, and I run over to let Sara-Beth and Leona in.

They are carrying platters of leftovers from the rehearsal dinner.

"We sent some with the boys but grabbed the sliders in case we got the munchies later," Sara-Beth explains.

Ansley and her mom join us, and Leona makes popcorn on the stove while Taeli signs in to her streaming service on the television.

"Okay, ladies, what do we want to watch first?" Taeli asks.

"*It's a Wonderful Life,*" Ansley chimes in.

"A classic. As the bride wishes," Taeli says as she types the title into the search bar.

Zoey grabs two fudge squares off one of the plates.

"Um, be careful with those," Maxi whispers.

Zoey looks down at the treats and back to Maxi. "Why? Do they have raisins in them or something?"

"Or something," I quip.

"Raisins? Who the hell would put a raisin in a brownie?" Jena asks.

Zoey shrugs.

"Leona's been known to slip a dash of medicinal herbs into her baked goods, if you know what I mean," Maxi explains.

"Oh. Ohhh," Zoey exclaims.

I stand up and call across the room, "Are these brownies spiked, or can we devour them?"

"If they have nuts, you can go nuts. If they're plain, one too many, and you'll go insane," Leona calls back, a mischievous grin on her face.

"Great. She's a stoner and a poet," Taeli groans.

Zoey examines the squares more closely and places one back on the plate.

"I'll just have one," she says and takes a tiny bite.

The credits roll on *It's a Wonderful Life*. I stand and offer everyone a beverage refill when I notice Maxi is crying.

"What's the matter?" I ask.

"I'm George Bailey."

"Huh?"

"I am. I've felt like an outsider my whole life, like I didn't matter to anyone, especially once my mom died. But here I am, having a baby, surrounded by you crazy, wonderful women who treat me like family. And I feel like I belong."

"That's because you do. You belong to Corbin, and that makes you ours too," Sara-Beth says.

"I should marry him," Maxi declares.

"Oh." Sara-Beth lets out a yelp.

"Like, before the baby comes, I should marry him."

"She should probably do it before she chickens out or changes her mind," I quip.

"I'll do it," Isley says.

"Do what?" Sara-Beth asks.

"I'll marry Corbin and Maxi."

"What? Now?" Maxi shrieks.

"Sure. Why not? We're all here," Isley says.

"Um, this is Ansley's wedding weekend," Maxi points out.

"So?" Ansley says.

Maxi turns to her. "So, we aren't hijacking your big day," Maxi exclaims.

"My big day is tomorrow. Tonight is wide open if you wanna claim it."

"We're in pajamas," Maxi mutters.

"Yeah, fancy silk pajamas," Brandee adds.

"What if he doesn't want to marry me?" Maxi whispers.

"Are you crazy? That man would have married you a year ago," Taeli bellows.

Maxi chews on her bottom lip. "I want Ansley at my wedding,

and I know Corbin would want Garrett there, and Ansley and Garrett can't see each other tonight."

"It's not like she's going to wear her gown. Isn't that what he's not supposed to see before the wedding?" Anna asks.

Ansley turns to her mother. "Mom?" she pleads.

Mrs. Humphries grabs the bottle from Leona and takes a huge swig.

"What the heck? I say you go for it!" she encourages.

"You're all insane," Maxi says.

"Tell us something we don't already know," Brandee muses.

"We don't have a marriage license."

"I'm the mayor. And in the state of Tennessee, a license is issued the same day. It might be after hours, but guess who can clock in anytime. In fact …" She pulls her phone out and taps at the screen. "Oh, look at that. I just did, and it's before midnight. Here, fill this out, and I'll approve it." She hands the phone to Maxi.

"I'll call Hilton and tell him we're coming to ambush the boys!" Sara-Beth squeals.

"Ansley, are you sure you're okay with this?" Maxi asks.

She beams. "Absolutely. I'd have you share the day with us and make it a double ceremony if I thought you'd want to."

"I'd rather be skinned alive than stand before two hundred people and a magazine crew."

"I know. So, let's go get you secretly married in that glass tower under the moon and stars."

"Am I really gonna do this?" Maxi asks.

"Why not?" I cry. "Let's go get you a husband."

Chapter
fourteen

I LEAD THE CHARGE TO THE OTHER SIDE OF THE HOTEL WITH ALL the girls in tow, except for little Annabelle. She fell asleep during the movie, and we carried her to bed and tucked her in for the night.

When we make it to the honeymoon suite, I knock, and when the door swings open, I push Maxi to the front.

Corbin is standing there with a confused expression, his father and brothers at his back.

"Maxi? What are you girls doing out here?" he asks.

Maxi looks over her shoulder at us.

"Go ahead," I encourage.

Maxi clears her throat and turns back to him. "You wanna get hitched?"

His eyebrows rise. "What?"

"You heard me," she barks.

He lets go of the door and steps into the hallway.

"Um, Maxi, sweetheart, you didn't drink anything, did you?" he asks under his breath.

"What? Of course not. I'm pregnant," she scoffs.

"You didn't get into any containers Leona brought?" he inquires further.

"I'm not high either."

He looks around at all our faces.

"Well? Don't leave me hanging. It's embarrassing," Maxi hisses.

"You're serious?"

"Yeah, Isley's taking care of the paperwork. And she can do the ceremony. So, if you want to get married, we can do it now, but I'd like to do it before midnight so we aren't stealing Ansley and Garrett's Christmas Eve wedding day."

Corbin processes the scene before him and tries to carefully assess Maxi's state of mind, and it's both amusing and kind of heart-wrenching.

He leans down and looks her in the eye. "I don't have a ring."

She smiles and shakes her head. "I don't need a ring. And I don't want months of planning and dress fittings and picking out stupid flowers."

She looks over her shoulder at Taeli and Ansley. "No offense."

Taeli shrugs. "None taken. It's not for everybody."

She looks back at Corbin. "My momma is gone. I don't have a father to walk me down the aisle. Lynn will forgive me. I'd rather spend the money and the time adding a nursery on the house and buying me a godforsaken minivan or something. So, I don't need a diamond. I just need you. If you want me."

He takes her face in his hands. "I want you more than anything in this world," he whispers.

"You two can use my and your father's bands," Sara-Beth offers as she takes her ring off.

"We couldn't," Maxi begins.

"Shush. Yes, you can. Our forty-fifth wedding anniversary is coming up, and we wanted to do something special. We'll get new bands."

Hilton slips his ring from his hand and offers it to Corbin. "Be honored to have you use the bands we used to commit ourselves to one another, son."

Corbin looks back at Garrett. "Are you good with this?"

Garrett grins. "Yeah, man. Hell, it's perfect timing. If you decided to elope last minute any other time, I'd likely be halfway across the world and have to miss it."

Maxi looks around. "I can't believe I'm still standing here, waiting for an answer."

"Yes, Miss Bufton. It would be my honor to marry you," Corbin shouts to the rafters.

"Switch pajamas with me," Ansley says as I braid Maxi's hair.

"No, these are fine," Maxi says.

"You need to be wearing the one that says *bride*, and I'll wear the one that says *bridesmaid*," Ansley insists.

Once I get the hair tie in place, Ansley's mom hands me a box.

"What's that?" Maxi asks.

"It's a tiara. I wore it on my wedding day, and I brought it just in case Ansley wanted to take her veil off at the reception. Now, I know I was guided to bring it for you."

Maxi begins to sob. "This is too much. It's all too much."

I walk around and kneel in front of her chair. "Maxi, sweetheart, it's not too much. It's just enough. I know you don't want some big to-do, but whether you realize it now or not, you're going to want to take pictures to remember this day. So you can show them to that baby when they ask about the day their mommy and daddy got married. So, wear the pajamas that say *bride*. Wear the tiara that intuition told Ansley's mother to bring. Accept the rings from Sara-Beth and Hilton and let us stand in the gap for your mother."

I take her face in my hands and wipe her tears. "She'd be so proud of you and so excited that you found a man who will love you and her grandchild the way you deserve to be loved."

Maxi nods. "She would love Corbin."

"I know she would."

"Will you give me away?" she asks.

"Oh, sweetheart, I'd be honored to do that for you and for your momma."

"Thank you."

"Okay, time's a-wastin', and you have a groom waiting for you who's gonna turn into a pumpkin at midnight," Erin says.

Maxi's eyes go wide. "How do I look?"

I place the crystal-encrusted crown on her head. "Perfect."

"Okay, I'm ready. Will one of you take my phone and call my sister and tell her what's going on? Then, we can FaceTime so she can watch us say *I do*."

Taeli walks over and picks her phone up from the table. "I got it."

"And I'm ready to video the whole thing," Erin says.

I take her hand and help her to her feet. Sara-Beth hands her a bouquet of poinsettias, white roses, red berries, and pine cones.

"It's beautiful. Where did you get it?" Maxi asks.

"I might have raided the reception centerpieces the florist sent over."

Maxi shakes her head and tries to give it back.

"They sent extras," Sara-Beth assures her.

"Oh."

Maxi raises the bouquet to her nose and smiles. She nods at me, and we lead her out to the elevator and up to the glass tower.

When the door opens, we see that the boys are already there.

They've lit dozens of candles and placed them all around the room that has been decorated for tomorrow's ceremony.

The girls rush past us to the altar, where Corbin waits in his own pair of dark blue silk pajamas with a red rose pinned to the lapel.

Garrett has his guitar in his hand, and he starts playing the bridal chorus as I walk Maxi down to her groom.

I place her hand in his and kiss both their cheeks before joining Sara-Beth and Hilton in the front row to watch our kiddos promise themselves to each other.

Sara-Beth and I are both a blubbering mess by the time Isley pronounces them husband and wife.

Corbin kisses his bride, and then he sweeps her up and tosses her over his shoulder in a fireman's hold and carries her down the aisle.

"Sorry, guys, but I'm out on the slumber party. I'm taking my wife to our room," he yells.

Maxi grins and waves.

We all cheer until they disappear behind the doors of the elevator.

"Well, the night sure took an unexpected turn," I say.

"It did indeed. I feel like we're on some kind of roll this weekend. Weston and Anna got engaged, Maxi is pregnant, and now, she and Corbin are married, and Garrett and Ansley are getting married tomorrow. And then it's Christmas. Does anybody else want in? Leona and Ralph?" Sara-Beth asks.

"We have to save something for Easter," I say.

"I wanna get married," Erin shouts.

"You're already married," Jena reminds her.

Erin pouts. "Oh, right."

"You should have a baby," Taeli suggests.

Erin scoffs. "The hell you say. I'm not built for children full-time. I'm made to be the fun aunt. The one who fills you up on chocolate and soda pop and sends you home. The one you can call to pick your drunk underage ass up from a party after sneaking out of your bedroom window. The one you know won't narc on you."

"Everyone does need one of those," I note.

"Yep, and every single one of these bitches' kiddos will have one," Erin agrees.

"Speaking of, I have a little flower girl sleeping that I need to get back to," Jena says.

"Right. Let's get back to our regularly scheduled night, shall we?" I suggest.

Ansley looks over at Garrett. "Meet back here tomorrow?"

"You'd better," he replies.

Garrett

I AWAKEN TO MY BROTHERS DRAGGING ME OUT OF BED. I KICK AT them as they carry me into the kitchen of the suite, where breakfast has been delivered by room service.

Corbin is part of the shenanigans.

"What the hell are you doing here? Shouldn't you still be worn out from your night with your new bride?" I ask.

He grins. "We got back to the room, I set her on the bed, and I went to run a bath in the jetted tub. By the time I made it back to her, she was fast asleep."

"No," Langford shouts.

"Yes," Corbin confirms.

"Damn, man, that's a disappointing wedding night," Weston quips.

Corbin shakes his head. "No, it wasn't. I held her all night while she slept. My wife and our baby that she's growing. It was the perfect night."

"Congratulations, man," I say.

"Thanks for sharing all this with me," he returns.

There is a knock at the door, and Pop answers. It's a photographer from the magazine.

"Hi, Aaron," I greet.

"Hi. I'm sorry to interrupt, but they want some candid shots of you guys getting ready."

I wave him in. "No problem."

"Great. You guys just do whatever and pretend like I'm not even here."

A thought of Ansley answering her door and having to invite a stranger inside flashes in my mind.

"I need to see Ansley," I say as I stand.

"You'll see her in a few hours," Morris says.

"No, I need to see her now."

"Dude, her mother will have your balls if you go marching over there, demanding to see Ansley," Weston says as he blocks the door.

"Move, West," I demand.

"Nope. Not gonna happen. If you absolutely have to talk to her, you can use your phone."

I stomp back to my bedroom and find my phone on the charger.

I take a seat on the bed and click her name.

"Hello?"

A symphony of voices starts chattering in the background.

"Garrett?"

"Hey, baby."

"Is everything okay?" she asks.

"Yeah, I just wanted to say that you don't have to do this."

She yells to the others that she needs a minute. Then, she comes back on the line.

"Are you having second thoughts?" she asks, and her voice cracks with emotion.

"Oh God, no, Ansley, baby," I reply.

"Then, what did you mean?"

"The photographer. I meant, you don't have to let the magazine's photographers barge in on you. I know we made the deal. At the time, I thought it was a good idea to keep the vultures at bay, but I wasn't considering how invasive it would feel to you. This day should be special and private."

"It is special. Nothing can change that," she says.

"Nothing," I agree.

"Besides, Tiny is nice. She's been drinking mimosas with us since seven o'clock. I'm not sure how great the photos will be, but I think we might have to set another place at Christmas dinner. Your mother and Leona are already trying to set her up with your cousin Leo."

Those crazy women.

"I should have known," I mutter.

She agrees.

"I can't wait to see you in your gown."

"Only a little while to go now," she says.

"I can't wait to see you out of your gown," I growl.

She giggles.

"I'll let you get back to getting ready," I say.

"Okay, I love you."

"I love you too, baby."

I click off the line and join the boys for celebratory shots.

I'm a bundle of nerves as I stand at the altar. I cup my hand and breathe into it to check my breath. I chewed a dozen mints before heading up here.

The last thing I need is Pastor Humphries smelling alcohol on me as I pledge myself to his daughter.

Fucking Weston and Morris.

I swear those two made it their mission to try and get me plastered on my wedding day.

Just wait until Weston's big day.

I make a mental commitment to show up the day of with several bottles of his favorite whiskey.

The harpist in the corner of the room starts to play as Ansley's friends appear and march down the aisle, one by one, led by little Annabelle as she tosses white rose petals in their path.

Once Erin is standing at the front, the music changes, and all the guests stand to their feet.

My manager and agent are front and center and grin in my direction as the doors swing open.

She's standing there, arm in arm with her father, who is about to burst with pride.

He has every right to be proud of his daughter. She's everything a man could want. Sweet, kind, funny, business savvy, self-assured, and sexy as hell.

I don't know why God allowed me to reclaim her heart, but I'll be eternally grateful.

Pastor Humphries leads her down the aisle to me and places her hand in mine.

"I'm trusting you with the most precious thing I have in the world, son," he says before kissing her cheek and walking around to stand in front of us.

"I've performed a lot of weddings in my day, and each one has been special, but this one … this one owns a piece of my heart. So, please forgive me if I get choked up," he begins.

"Garrett and Ansley have chosen to write their own vows, so I'm going to let them speak their hearts now. Garrett, son, go ahead."

I swallow hard as her gorgeous eyes gaze at me in anticipation.

"Ansley, baby, I sat down at my desk with a blank sheet of paper a dozen times and tried to write my vows. To put down in a few sentences how much you agreeing to hitch your wagon to mine for eternity means to me. But the words wouldn't come. I just sat there, staring at a blank page. Then, I spotted my guitar leaning against the wall, and as you know, I'm used to expressing my feelings through song lyrics. So, here goes," I say as my father walks up to the altar with my guitar in his hands.

"Thanks, Pop," I tell him as I take the instrument and strum a few chords.

The soft, melodic twang of the strings fills the room, and an audible gasp from the bridal party adds to the beauty of the music.

With a deep breath, I begin to turn my feelings into words.

"From the moment we met, I knew my life had changed for the better," I croon as the memories of our teenage angst and our adult journey back to one another flood my mind.

I close my eyes and continue pouring my heart and soul into each verse.

"You're the dawn to my darkest nights, the strength that carries me higher, and the love that fills my heart to overflowing."

I open my eyes and smile as hers sparkle with unshed tears, and she laughs.

"Your touch can calm even the stormiest of days."

I choke up as I think about the future we're about to embark on.

"I promise to cherish you, to stand by your side, and to be your rock when life gets tough. It's me and you standing true through life's ups and downs, my Tennessee mountain queen," I sing, my voice cracking with emotion.

"I promise to love you with all that I am and all that I will ever be as our love story continues to unfold, love of my life, Ansley Marie, my beautiful Tennessee mountain queen."

I whisper the final words to her; they are a promise from my heart to hers, a commitment, and a declaration of love that will bind us together for a lifetime.

I set the guitar aside as Pastor Humphries clears his throat.

"Ansley?"

She looks from me to her father, and she sniffles. He gives her a reassuring wink, and her eyes come back to me.

"How am I supposed to follow that, you big jerk?" she asks.

I chuckle, as does the rest of the room.

"Try," I encourage.

She closes her eyes and takes a deep breath. When she opens them, she smiles at me.

"I've been dreaming about this moment since I was a young girl, and I honestly can't believe we are finally here. As I stand at this altar with you, in front of all the people we love, my heart is racing with anticipation. Just like it did the day we met. I knew that my life was never going to be the same, and I didn't want it to be. I want a life full of adventure with you, Garrett Tuttle. I promise to be your confidant, your partner in crime, and your biggest fan as we face the challenges life brings our way and celebrate the joys yet to come," she says, her voice quivering with emotion.

I clasp her fingers tighter as I fight back my own tears.

"I promise to cherish you, to encourage you, and to love you unconditionally through all the seasons of life," she vows, her eyes locking with mine and glistening with happiness.

"As I stand here today, in front of you and our loved ones in this gorgeous snow globe, I pledge to always be your biggest fan, and your greatest love," she concludes, and I swear my heart almost bursts with love for this woman.

Our friends and family cheer with delight, their presence a reminder of the support that surrounds us.

We aren't just joining our lives together; we are weaving them into a beautiful story of love and commitment that includes everyone in this room.

Pastor Humphries leans forward. "I think you did just fine, kiddo," he whispers to his daughter before standing back up and addressing Weston and Erin. "Do we have the rings?"

My hands tremble as we exchange the bands.

"By the power vested in me, I now pronounce you husband and wife. You may seal your vows with a kiss," he announces.

I take her face into my hands and kiss her with all that I have.

We are lost in each other when the catcalls begin.

"Jeez, let her up for air," Morris's voice booms.

Our mouths break apart.

"Congratulations, Mrs. Tuttle," I whisper against her lips.

Not to be outdone by Corbin, I dip down and scoop her into my arms and proceed to carry her down the aisle.

Her joyous laughter rings out and fills the air around us.

Chapter

sixteen

Ansley

THE SUN DIPS BELOW THE HORIZON, CASTING A WARM ORANGE glow across the panoramic view of the snowy mountaintops of Balsam Ridge. We take in the beauty from the glass tower, where our wedding reception is in full swing.

As I stand here, hand in hand with my new husband, I can't help but feel overwhelmed by the love and joy that surround us.

The laughter of our friends and the chatter of our families fill the air, a beautiful symphony mixing with the music from Garrett's band.

The scent of freshly cut flowers mingles with the delicious aroma of the buffet that was set up under the twinkling fairy lights strung across the ceiling.

I steal a glance at Garrett as he talks to our guests, and my heart swells with love. I didn't think it was possible to love him more than I did yesterday, but somehow, it feels different now.

He is mine, and I am his.

His eyes sparkle as he laughs at something one of his Nashville friends said.

Ever the superstar, his strong, confident presence makes me feel safe and cherished.

"Ansley, can I steal you away for a moment?" Maxi asks.

I nod and follow her to a quieter corner of the room.

"What's up, Maxi?" I ask, curious.

She leans in and whispers, "I have something special for you."

She places the antique tiara on my head.

I ditched the long, cumbersome veil as soon as the ceremony was over.

I carefully adjust the delicate crown as I fight back tears.

"It's the tiara your grandmother and mother wore on their wedding days," she says. "It belongs on your head tonight. Thank you for letting me borrow it and the love and family it represents."

I'm touched beyond words that she returned it to me. My grandmother was a source of inspiration for me, and I wish she could have been here to see me walk down the aisle. This heirloom feels like a precious connection to her.

"Thank you, Maxi," I say, hugging her tightly. "You are a part of our love and family. We're sisters now."

She releases me, takes a step back, and looks around at the others, who are being arranged and rearranged by the photographers at the moment.

"Oh my God, we are. I just gained five brothers and five sisters," Maxi gasps.

"And a set of lovable and wise parents," Sara-Beth says as she comes up behind us.

"And the best nephews in the whole wide world," Tucker, who is by her side, adds.

"This is wild," Maxi mutters.

Tucker approaches her and sticks out his elbow.

"May I have this dance, Aunt Maxi?" he asks.

"Sure, kid. Let's see what you got," she accepts.

Sara-Beth watches them disappear into the sea of bodies on the dance floor, and then she turns to me.

"How are you holding up?" she asks.

"I'm kind of rethinking the gorgeous blue shoes at the moment," I admit.

She winks and reaches down into the pocket of her mother's gown—both she and Mom insisted theirs have pockets—and produces a pair of fur-lined white satin slippers.

I gasp. "You're the best mother-in-law a girl could ever hope for!"

I take them from her, hobble over to one of the tables, and take a seat. I discreetly remove the beautiful but vicious stilettos, hide them under the table, and step into the heavenly clouds.

"Ahh," I moan.

"You keep making that sound, and we aren't going to make it to the cake cutting," Garrett's deep voice says, and his warm breath tickles my ear.

I turn to see him standing with two flutes of champagne.

"Oh, I'm not missing that cake, Mr. Tuttle," I quip.

He sets the glasses on the table and offers his hand. "Dance with me, wife."

I let him lead me onto the dance floor, and the band begins the intro to the first song he ever wrote for me, "Tennessee Sunsets." He holds me in his arms and sings the lyrics in my ear, and I close my eyes. Even though I know the room is filled with hundreds of bodies, it feels like we're the only ones here.

This moment is perfect.

It's the one I'll commit to memory and carry in my heart forever.

When the song ends, Garrett kisses my neck and continues to circle us around the floor. I open my eyes as the next song begins, and he is staring down at me.

"Are you happy, baby?"

I nod. "Are you?" I ask.

"I'll be happier when they finally cut that damn cake so I can get you out of this dress."

I sigh and lean my forehead against his chin. "I'll be happy when they cut that dang cake too."

We look to our side and see Caleb, handsome as can be in his suit and tie, guiding Annabelle around the dance floor as she stomps on his feet.

"Hang in there, buddy," Garrett says as he reaches over and taps his back.

Caleb rolls his eyes and continues to take her missteps like a man.

The tempo picks up, and Erin and her husband, Ted, boogie past us.

"Those photographers finally cut us loose," she calls.

Weston glides by us as he twirls a giggling Kaela in the air.

The rest of the bridal party join us, and we all start swinging each other around as we laugh and sing at the top of our lungs.

Leona and Ralph and Sara-Beth and Hilton even give us all a quick shagging tutorial.

When the band announces they are taking a short break so the bride and groom can cut the wedding cake, Garrett lets out a loud shout and grabs my hand.

The exquisite wedding cake stands four tiers tall, each layer adorned with red berry branches and edible flowers. The base tier is covered in a textured buttercream frosting, resembling the rugged bark of a tree, giving it that authentic rustic charm.

The top tier is covered in a semi-naked frosting, allowing hints of the delicious cake layers to peek through, and is topped by a pair of lovebirds, perched on a delicate spun-sugar nest.

It's almost too pretty to cut.

Almost.

We wait for everyone to gather around, and then we take hold of the knife together and slice into the luscious sponge. Then, we try to shove it down each other's throat while everyone cheers and snaps pictures, as is tradition.

Garrett kisses the frosting from the tip of my nose and then raises his glass in a toast, and everyone falls silent.

"I want to thank every one of you for being here with us. Our parents, who worked tirelessly to help us perfect every detail. My brothers and their families, for filling the day with joy. My band, for rocking the wedding-singer vibe. And my bride, Ansley," he says, his voice filled with emotion, "the love of my life and my partner in this incredible journey. I'm so grateful you chose me to be your husband, and I can't wait to see what the future holds for us."

Tears well up in my eyes as I raise my glass in response, and the room erupts into cheers and applause.

The rest of the evening passes in a blur of laughter, dancing, and heartfelt conversations. We are surrounded by love, and it feels like the stress and worry of the world have faded away.

It might have taken us three decades to get here, but my heart still races for that green-eyed boy who bloodied Toby Ballard's nose under the bleachers in our seventh grade PE class.

"Wait right there." Garrett hops out of the truck and sprints around the hood to get to my door.

"What are you doing?"

"Carrying my new bride across the threshold," he says as he plucks me from the passenger seat and hip-bumps the door closed.

As soon as we make it up the steps and in the front door, he sets me on my feet, and his large hands settle on my hips. He kicks the door shut as he turns me and leads us into the living room.

His mouth finds mine immediately, and he hungrily kisses me as he walks me backward to the leather couch in front of the roaring fire.

"How did you get a fire started?" I ask between his kisses.

"Weston left before us and ran by to get it started," he says as his hands slide down and around to cup my behind and bring me in closer.

"That was thoughtful of him," I say, and I help him gather the skirt of my gown and wrap my legs around his waist as he slowly lowers us to the couch and comes over the top of me.

My head falls back against the cool leather of the armrest, and I reach and thread my fingers through his silky, dark hair and tug. He presses his body into mine, and the evidence of his need pulses against my stomach.

"I've been dying to get you out of this thing all night, and now, I don't know where to start," he growls as he fumbles with the tulle.

I bear up and twist, exposing my back.

"Fuck, that's a lot of buttons," he says.

His shaky fingers start at the top and plucks at the satin-covered buttons.

Frustrated, he starts yanking them loose. Several fall and ping against the hardwood floor.

"Garrett," I cry.

"I'll pay to have the whole damn thing resewn," he says as he continues to pry them from my back. As the last one gives way, I turn to face him.

The warmth of the fire and the heat of him envelop me, and I start trembling with need. I decide I'm fine with that plan, so I plant my right foot and push up, trying desperately to get closer to him as he peels the gown down my body.

I arch my back, and the starch of his dress shirt scratches across my aching breasts. I slide my hands from his hair and down his back, the tips of my fingers digging into his muscles.

He lets out a guttural moan as his mouth runs down the column of my throat, sucking and nipping as he makes his way to my chest.

The need pulses through me, and I want to touch and kiss every inch of him.

I grip him tighter as his tongue explores the tops of my breasts that are exposed. An exquisite tingle shoots straight down my spine as he sucks a nipple between his teeth.

God, that feels so good.

I sigh my encouragement as I fight to free the hem of his shirt from his tux slacks.

He brings his head up at the sound, and before I have a chance to complain, he leans up and yanks the shirt and tosses it to the floor.

I bear up and take his mouth as I slide his zipper down slowly.

He is hard and ready as I reach in to release him from his boxer briefs.

I hold the base of him with one hand as I stroke him firmly with the other. Running the white-tipped nail of my finger down the hard ridges. He twitches in my grip, and his breath catches as he watches me.

"Ansley," he rasps as his hands drop to my shoulders and grip me tightly.

"Yes, husband?" I whisper.

"I'm going to make love to you on every surface in the house before the night's over."

I dart my tongue out and lick his bottom lip as I continue to stroke him.

"Promises, promises," I murmur, and the heat in his eyes as he watches me almost melts me into the leather.

He groans, and his hands fist my hair and tug gently. I fall back to the couch.

I mutter unintelligible words as his mouth finds my breasts again. I can sense that he is holding on to his control as best he can as he takes his time kissing his way down my body at a maddeningly leisurely pace. Stroking and caressing every exposed inch of skin until I'm a desperate, writhing mess.

When he reaches my thighs, he presses them apart.

He growls low and deep in his throat when he finds me wet and ready for him. He rakes his fingertip through my folds and then brings it to his lips and sucks.

I watch his face as he looks at me, bared to him. His breath quickens as he spreads me with his fingers, and his tongue starts to explore my hot flesh.

I arch up as I cling to him.

"Garrett," I moan.

Desire ripples down my spine as I watch him devour me. Claiming me in a way that feels new.

He nips at my clit with his teeth, and my hips jump in his hold.

Every nerve ending in my body ignites, and pleasure twists and knots inside of me as he inserts a finger and starts to curl it in and out.

He takes his time using his mouth, tongue, and hands to drive me into a frenzy.

I sink my fingers into his scalp and keep him where I need him as I raise my hips to meet his tongue until I am shaking beneath him.

He brings his eyes to mine and holds my stare as he moves on top of me.

"I want to be inside you when you come for me the first time, Mrs. Tuttle."

I cry out as he enters me with one swift thrust of his hips. Filling me completely.

"Yes!"

He reaches back and clasps one of my legs and guides it over his hip so he can move deeper, faster, and my head presses into the armrest as I grip the sides of the sofa.

He bends his head so he can kiss my exposed neck, and the sensation of his gentle kiss, in contrast to his pounding rhythm, is just what I need.

His breath starts coming in short, hard pants as my leg locks tightly around his waist.

"Baby," he grunts as my muscles tighten around him.

I slide my hands down his sides to the curves of his ass and hold on.

He starts making those husky, guttural noises that let me know he is close to the edge as well.

I'm so close myself and desperate for release when he slips one hand between us, touching me in just the right spot. That does it. My body begins to convulse as I hoarsely scream his name.

He follows me to the edge as his pleasure explodes inside me as my own climax takes him over.

We lie here, tangled together as the warmth of the fire dries our sweat-slick bodies.

"Want to take a shower with me and tackle surface number two?" I ask.

He grins, and that damn dimple gives me my answer.

Hilton

SARA-BETH AND I SIT BY THE TWINKLING CHRISTMAS TREE AS our six sons and their families gather in the cozy ballroom at Langford's resort.

She and the girls went all out in order to bring the feeling of home to Misty Mountain this year.

Graham and Taeli, Corbin and Maxi, Langford and Isley, Weston and Anna, Morris and Zoey, and even the honeymooners showed up for Christmas breakfast on this special morning.

Our hearts swell with joy as we see our grandchildren—Tucker, Caleb, and Kaela—eagerly tearing open the presents Santa left under the large tree.

The room is filled with laughter and the warmth of family love. This is what Christmas is all about.

Sara-Beth sits on the floor to help Anna with one of Kaela's boxes, and Weston takes the seat beside me.

"A lot has changed since last Christmas, Pop."

I nod my head, knowing that a lot changes every year.

"I've seen many Christmases come and go, son, and believe me, there are days I feel every single year of life in my bones. But in my mind, I'm still a boy. One who gets a thrill every time your momma smiles at me. It happens so fast. Too fast. One day, you're riding around on your lawn mower with your son in your lap, helping you steer, and the next day, that same son has his own boy riding the mower with him."

I bring my eyes to him. "Soak up every moment in between."

He nods. "I will, Pop."

Kaela lets out a frustrated wail when the girls are unable to free the doll from its packaging.

"I think that's my cue," Weston says as he pulls a pocketknife from his jeans and hops to the rescue.

Corbin helps Sara-Beth back to her feet, and she comes back to me.

"Look what we made," she says as she lays her head against my shoulder.

"Are you happy, Mrs. Tuttle?" I ask my bride.

She looks up at me, her eyes full of joyful tears. "My cup runneth over."

The End

acknowledgments

Well, that's a wrap!

All the residents of Balsam Ridge are happily living their lives, having babies, and building empires.

I dedicated this one to you, the readers, because it is truly my love letter to you all. A cherry on top of this series that has captured my heart and hopefully yours as well.

I'm excited to jump into new waters in the coming year with the Sandcastle Cove Series.

If you want a sneak peek into what's to come, you'll find it in the short story I contributed to *Aloha: An Anthology for Maui.*

As always, it takes a small village to get the stories from my page to your hands. And I have the best village in publishing standing with me. From my crazy-talented cover designer, Sommer Stein, who always takes my breath away; to my amazing formatter, Stacey Blake; my eagle-eyed proofreader, Judy Zweifel; and my long-suffering and ever-gracious editor, Jovana Shirley, who never makes me grovel for long and always rescues me. Thank you, Jo, for your skill, patience, and friendship. (Commas are still the devil.)

Each one of these women plays a pivotal role in my success, and they are invaluable to me. My uncertain schedule never makes it easy for them. I'm so blessed that they keep me. I wouldn't want to publish a book without them.

Autumn Sexton, my amazing publicist and one of my dearest friends. You are my rock and sounding board and late-night plotting partner. I love you to the moon, and you are stuck with me till death do us part. Thank you so much.

And last but not least, yet again, thank you to my Miller for being my anchor and the best life partner a girl could ask for. You're truly the flesh-and-blood book boyfriend every girl dreams of. I love you more.

other books

Cross My Heart Duet

Both of Me

Both of Us

Poplar Falls

Rustic Hearts

Stone Hearts

Wicked Hearts

Fragile Hearts

Merry Hearts

Crazy Hearts

Knitted Hearts

Lake Mistletoe Series

Lake Mistletoe

Smitten in Lake Mistletoe

Stranded in Lake Mistletoe

The Balsam Ridge Series

Life After Wife

Fate After Fame

Rain After Fire

Hope After Loss

Rise After Fall

Cozy After Snow

About
the author

Amber Kelly is a romance author that calls North Carolina home. She has been a avid reader from a young age and you could always find her with her nose in a book completely enthralled in an adventure. With the support of her husband and family, in 2018, she decided to finally give a voice to the stories in her head and her debut novel, Both of Me was born. You can connect with Amber on Facebook at facebook.com/AuthorAmberKelly, on IG @authoramberkelly, on twitter @AuthorAmberKel1 or via her website www.authoramberkelly.com..